NEITHER OF T
THE MOMENT

He grabbed for S
exuberant hug. "

"We've found it." Shane wrapped her arms
around him, thinking only of the thrill of
discovery they were sharing. In a giddy kiss of
triumph her lips met his.

Then all at once suppressed desire took over,
ripping through them with the swiftness of a
prairie fire. The relics forgotten, Dirk's mouth
settled hungrily on Shane's parted lips.
Possessed by the most intense craving of her
life, she wound her arms around his neck.
His heated skin filled her nostrils with erotic
perfume; his tongue teased her face, her
neck, as he peeled away her shirt. And he
knelt before her, bare and golden. "I want
you, Shane. . . ."

LISA ST. JOHN has lived in the Southwest all her life, but
her travels have taken her throughout the United States
and to many other parts of the world. She is married.
When she is not writing, she enjoys bird-watching and
reading. Her books have been published in nine foreign
countries. She is the author of another Rapture Romance,
Gossamer Magic.

Dear Reader:

It's a new Rapture! Starting this month we'll be bringing you only the best four books each month, by well-known favorite authors and exciting new writers, and to demonstrate our commitment to quality we've created a new look for Rapture: bigger, bolder, brighter. But don't judge our books by their covers—open them up and read them. We've used the comments and opinions we've heard from *you*, the reader, to make our selections, and we know you'll be delighted.

Keep writing to us. Your letters have already helped us bring you better books—the kind you want—and we depend on them. Of course, we are always happy to forward mail to our authors—writers need to hear from their fans!

And don't miss any of the inside story on Rapture. To tell you about upcoming books, introduce you to the authors, and give you a behind-the-scenes look at romance publishing, we've started a *free* newsletter, *The Rapture Reader*. Just write to the address below, and we will be happy to send you each issue.

Happy reading!

The Editors
Rapture Romance
New American Library
1633 Broadway
New York, NY 10019

STARFIRE

by

Lisa St. John

RAPTURE ROMANCE
NEW AMERICAN LIBRARY

PUBLISHER'S NOTE
This novel is a work of fiction. Names, characters, places, and incidents either are the product of the author's imagination or are used fictitiously, and any resemblance to actual persons, living or dead, events, or locales is entirely coincidental.

NAL BOOKS ARE AVAILABLE AT QUANTITY DISCOUNTS
WHEN USED TO PROMOTE PRODUCTS OR SERVICES.
FOR INFORMATION PLEASE WRITE TO PREMIUM MARKETING DIVISION,
NEW AMERICAN LIBRARY, 1633 BROADWAY,
NEW YORK, NEW YORK 10019.

SIGNET, SIGNET CLASSIC, MENTOR, PLUME, MERIDIAN and NAL BOOKS
are published by New American Library,
1633 Broadway, New York, New York 10019

First Printing, March, 1984

1 2 3 4 5 6 7 8 9

PRINTED IN THE UNITED STATES OF AMERICA

Chapter One

❧

Shane McBride drew in her mount and listened to the whir of a light plane approaching through the peach-colored sky from the direction of the Georgia coast. After a few moments, the craft came into view and dropped down on the beach a hundred yards ahead of her, alarming the Appaloosa mare she sat astride. Ten days on the island had taught her that an arrival of any kind was a major event, and while she calmed the mare, she watched eagerly as the door on the plane's passenger side opened and a man climbed down.

He was tall, Shane saw, lean and athletic-looking in the early-morning light, with dark hair that twisted in the wind stirred by the plane's propellers. Faded jeans hugged his narrow hips and a white business shirt, open past his throat, revealed more dark hair. He caught the duffel bag that was tossed after him and then, with a careless salute, he stepped back and watched the plane take off.

Shane gave him a minute to adjust to his surroundings and then she cantered over, her brown eyes sparkling a welcome that was as naturally friendly as the smile that lit her face.

In her soft Southwestern drawl she greeted him. "Welcome to Wanatoka. May I offer you a ride up to the house?"

The Dirksen Foundation Center for Scientific Research, housed in a magnificent brick mansion, was the only real center of activity on the island, and she was certain that this craggy-featured man whose dark eyes were frankly examining every curve of her lithe young body was—like herself—one of its endowed scholars.

While she talked, she eyed him curiously, wondering what his field might be. All the historians she had met so far had indoorish pallors and wore button-down collars and coats, even in the library. The geologists invariably stomped about in boots and smoked pipes, and the men from the Institute of Ecology carried smart leather briefcases, not well-worn duffel bags.

"The house isn't far," she went on. "But a number of paths cross in the undergrowth. You might get lost if you try to walk it."

He leveled a languid gaze on her. "I doubt that." Nevertheless, he set his foot in the stirrup Shane's own foot had vacated and swung himself up behind her. Before she realized he was settled, the darkly handsome newcomer dug his knees into the mare's side and they started off at a brisk trot toward the thick growth of moss-hung oaks that lined the beach.

Wanatoka, one of the small sea islands in the barrier chain dotting the Georgia coast, lay a scant twenty miles off the mainland, but its insular way of life made it seem to Shane a thousand miles from the modern world. Sleepy Sicilian donkeys trod the paths through the undergrowth, carrying on their backs firewood for the black natives whose ancestors had been among the first slaves brought to North America. All manner of wildlife—including bighorn goats, turkeys, and the alarmingly ferocious razorback hogs—roamed at will. There were no telephones, no television sets, and no newspapers, except twice a week when a boat went into Savannah for supplies and mail, and to pick up whoever might be waiting on the dock. Until a few minutes before when the blue-and-white Cessna set down, Shane had assumed that the mail boat was the only way to get to the island. But another glance at the hard-packed sand told her that at low tide the narrow beach made a perfect landing strip.

Across her shoulder, she chatted agreeably. "I wish I'd been smart enough to think of a plane. The day I came out, the sea was awful! I turned green as grass before we even lost sight of the shore."

"If you don't like water," the man holding on to her waist observed tonelessly, "you shouldn't have come here."

Shane's voice cooled. "I love water. But I don't like pitching power boats."

Every morning since her arrival she had saddled the mare and come down for a dawn ride out into the surf. The returning tide turned gold and silver as they frolicked in it. Gulls wheeled and squalled, and the air was as clear as a crystal ball. She always came back to start the day's work as fresh as the shy violets that bloomed along the forest trails.

Feeling charitable again, and hungry all at once, she commented, "You don't know how lucky you are. You've arrived just in time for one of the most marvelous breakfasts you've ever had in your life."

But once again her companion rebuffed her. "I had breakfast hours ago." He yawned then, noisily and at length, making no effort to excuse himself, though the curling tendrils at the back of Shane's neck danced in the warm breath he exhaled.

Thinking darkly that his rudeness had ruined her morning, Shane slapped the reins on the mare's neck and they rode in silence the rest of the way to the mansion. Lulled by the jolting rhythm of the horse's gait, the stranger behind her hung on to her and dozed placidly, apparently thinking of nothing at all.

Throughout the day Shane expected to reencounter her disagreeable riding companion. Certainly she expected him to appear for meals, but at noon she sat down alone in the Center's vast oak-paneled dining room. The gray-brick mansion seemed to have swallowed him up the moment he slid down from her horse.

The large rambling house held accommodations for six guests, but apparently because of the upcoming Easter holidays, everyone except Shane had departed on the midweek mail boat. Hailing from New Mexico and still enrolled as a graduate student at the University of Texas, Shane thought both places that she called home were too distant to be worth the trip, and so for the past few days she had been the only pampered guest at the island hideaway.

The mansion that housed the Center was more like a luxurious hotel than a spot set aside for serious study. A competent staff served unobtrusively, anticipating every guest's need and meeting it immediately. Originally the house had been the winter home of Abraham Dirksen, an early pioneer in the development of the telephone and telegraph. But in recent years, through a clause in the will of one of his descendants, house and island had been incorporated into a foundation designed to provide a comfortable retreat for study by worthy individuals interested in exploring and preserving the island's unique assets and availing themselves of the Foundation's marvelous library.

According to the brochures Shane had pored over before applying for her grant to study Wanatoka's Indian burial mounds, the original Dirksen was one of a score of Eastern millionaires who migrated as winter residents to the

Georgia coast in the late 1800s. Most of them had settled on Jekyl Island to the south, forming an elite enclave for three generations, but Dirksen, apparently something of an eccentric, had preferred an island all to himself.

The home he built was on the southern end of Wanatoka. The upper levels of the castlelike structure held half a dozen sleeping apartments, several single bedrooms, and numerous baths. On the lower level, a minstrel's gallery looked down on a vast, beamed living room. There was an extensive library and a solarium filled with exotic plants as well as an impressive collection of shells. A fully equipped kitchen, a sunny breakfast room, and the large formal dining room where Shane picked at her solitary meals completed the first floor.

Outside, a clipped, carefully tended lawn and garden surrounded the house, but the rest of the island remained in its original wild state. Its only permanent inhabitants were a scanty population of blacks whose ancestors had preceded Abraham Dirksen's arrival and who, to Dirksen's credit, had always been regarded as sovereign citizens whose rights were strictly observed.

It was an ideal spot to complete research for the master's thesis in archaeology that Shane was attempting, and she had easily adapted to the relaxed pace of the island. She appreciated, too, the foremost rule laid down by the Foundation, which stipulated that each endowed scholar be guaranteed the privacy to work without interruption. Only at mealtimes and from seven until nine in the evening were the guests permitted to congregate socially. The rule provided each participant the necessary time for study and it also prevented any bores among them from imposing themselves in an environment from which there was no escape.

Until the others, with whom she had barely gotten acquainted, unexpectedly departed, Shane had gotten along very well with the relative isolation. She welcomed it, in fact. She rose eagerly each morning for her ride down to the surf at dawn. The rest of the day she spent studying the ancient burial mounds scattered over the island, reading and writing in the library, and during periods of relaxation, exploring the mysteries of the primeval, moss-festooned forest that lay on every side.

After two days of dining alone at the long oak table and sipping coffee afterward in a living room that could easily hold twenty, Shane discovered just how eagerly she was looking forward to conversation with the island's latest arrival, no matter how taciturn and rude he had been that morning.

When at half-past-eight that evening he still hadn't appeared, she questioned Saphirra, the young native girl who was serving her coffee. "What's happened to the gentleman who arrived earlier? Are you sure he's aware of the meal schedule?"

The girl smiled. "Oh, yes, missa." Her soft

island dialect was a charming blend of ancient African and English. "Misser Holland hab food bah stair."

"Sent up to his room, do you mean?" Shane's brown eyes opened wide. No one was allowed the privilege of being served dinner privately. Unless for some reason one wasn't able to come down. "He isn't ill, is he?"

"Not ill." The girl's eyes took on a compassionate, buttery look. "Poor Misser Holland bahd tired. Is lay down for resting. Byhap tomorrow come down." And she padded away in the soft woven hemp slippers most of the islanders wore.

Poor Mr. Holland indeed! Shane sat on, fuming by the fire. Who did he think he was, flouting the rules on his very first day? He might think no one was around to make him heed them, but he was sadly mistaken. Frances Forester, the Center's starchy director, would soon set him straight. The stocky, middle-aged Miss Forester had quarters separate from the main building. She was primarily a business manager and generally kept in the background, but her presence kept things running smoothly and she strictly enforced the policies set up by the Foundation. Shane had seen her display her firm efficiency on one occasion and she was sure the formidable lady would appreciate being informed that a malingerer had come into their midst.

However, when Shane rose the next morning, she smiled at the tattletale nastiness she had contemplated the evening before. She had indulged in such foolishness because she was lonely. And she had resented it when Holland whoever-he-was had failed to meet her expectations. How childish, she thought, to be peeved over such a trifle. What she needed was to get busy minding her own business.

While she pulled on her jeans, hurrying because the sun was already climbing in the sky, she mapped out a rigorous schedule for the day. A ride first. Then breakfast. Afterward she'd ask for a box lunch and a Jeep, and spend the rest of her time at the other end of the island, excavating a mound she had begun work on the week before. By nightfall she'd be too weary to worry about talking to anyone.

She grinned impishly at her reflection in the mirror. She might even save back part of her lunch for eating later in her room. If Holland did happen to show up for dinner, he could see how *he* liked sitting alone at a table twelve feet long!

Shane and her mare had been frolicking in the surf for only a few minutes when the mare's ears lifted. Whinnying, she ignored Shane's tug on the reins and instead wheeled around toward the shore. Coming into the water astride a chestnut-colored stallion was the man Saphirra had called Holland. Rested at last, Shane thought grimly. And now he's come down to spoil another morning for me.

But the look he gave her as he approached was

pleasant enough, and she couldn't help noticing, too, how well he sat his horse. Instead of the white business shirt he had worn the day before, a gray Shetland pullover covered his broad chest, its softness contrasting agreeably with the strong, male lines of his body. Shane found herself tugging self-consciously at the frayed collar of her faded polo shirt. It was her favorite costume for digs, but its bilious green color was hardly flattering.

"Scouting more planes?" he commented idly when he had reined in his horse beside her.

"Hardly. Yours is the only one I've seen since I came here." Her throat was tight, but she was pleased that none of her tension showed in her voice. "I think we're off-limits for airliners."

His dark-eyed glanced drifted over the slender lines of her body. "That's one of Wanatoka's charms, isn't it? The silence?" Then abruptly he put out his hand. "I'm Dirk Holland. I think I owe you an apology."

"Shane McBride," she answered. The hand that grasped hers enclosed it in a curiously caressing manner. Those dark eyes were blue, she saw. How had she failed to notice that before? "An apology for what?"

He let go of her hand slowly. "I'm sure you've met grizzly bears who were more agreeable than I was yesterday."

She kept her gaze steady. "Only one or two."

He laughed, causing the skin around his eyes to crinkle appealingly. "You'll have to forgive me. The only time I snarl that impressively is when I've flown in nonstop from the Orient and missed my connection in San Francisco."

"Oh, I see." Jet lag. That was reasonable, wasn't it? She relaxed a little, eyeing him curiously. "Were you working on a grant in the East too?"

"What?"

"A grant." Her lips curved in a teasing smile. "If you can't recall what that is, you must still be badly fogged up. Were you in the Orient studying? What's your field?"

"My field is communications. And now that you mention it, I suppose it's correct to say that studying is what I was doing in Hong Kong." The sensuous mouth that she couldn't stop looking at twisted in a wry grin. "Though at the time it seemed more like a chess game."

"I'm sorry," Shane murmured. "I don't follow you."

"It doesn't matter." His strong, broad palm smoothed the stallion's mane. "Let's ride. We can talk later."

Shane waited for him to move past her, but the mare was eager to follow and before long she felt comfortable with the dark-haired man beside her. He seemed as captivated as she by the golden tide swirling up to the horses' bellies, foaming and sliding past, only to rush back in a moment to soak their jeans again with warm saltwater.

Shane had never ventured so far from shore

before and she wondered if the sandy seabed might not suddenly drop off into an Atlantic abyss. But her companion showed no hesitation. His daring gave the impression that he knew the underwater topography of Wanatoka's beaches, and inspired by his confidence, she gave herself over to pure enjoyment.

Moving back toward the shore a few minutes later, they paused to savor the power of the waves swaying the mounts beneath them, and Dirk further impressed her by pointing out a great blue heron and several teal loons that were winging their way inland.

"If you're only a communications expert," she said, mocking him good-naturedly, "I'm surprised that you're so well-informed about herons and loons." The wind, teasing her curly brown hair, brought flattering spots of color to her tanned cheeks. But she was too absorbed in watching the birds' graceful flight to notice that Dirk Holland was absorbed in watching her.

He said quietly, "Anyone from around here knows seabirds."

"Oh—" She turned back and saw how intently he was studying her. The color in her cheeks spread. Those marvelous eyes . . . violet almost. They could see straight through one.

"Oh," she said again. "I didn't realize this was your part of the country. Everyone here seems to be from somewhere else. I just assumed—"

He finished for her. "That I was a foreigner too? You're from New Mexico, aren't you?" His even, white teeth showed in a smile. "I expected you to be a man, you know."

Shane's lips parted in bewilderment. "What? What do you mean?"

"Shane." He lifted his shoulders. "It's a man's name."

She bristled. "Obviously it isn't." The assumption annoyed her. "There's a well-known woman columnist named Shane. And several movie actresses, too."

"Really?" Amusement played at the corners of his lips. Lips she wanted to kiss, Shane realized suddenly.

Her gaze wavered. "Besides, how could you have speculated? Did you ask someone what my name was?"

Saphirra was who she had in mind, but he astonished her by answering, "Your name was on a list that was sent to me."

"You were sent a list of who would be studying here?" Shane blinked. "Why wasn't I sent one?"

He answered calmly, "Perhaps because it wasn't your responsibility to decide who would be asked to leave and who allowed to stay."

The horses came out on the shore, shaking water from their coats as Shane stared in amazement at her riding companion. "What are you talking about?"

He prodded his stallion into an ambling gait across the sand. The mare followed, nuzzling the stallion's side. "I'm afraid you've jumped to the wrong conclusion about me. I am not, as you supposed, here on a temporary grant." Amusement flickered in his eyes. "The island," he said evenly, "belongs to me."

Shane's jaw dropped.

"Dirk is short for Dirksen. My paternal grandmother was Abraham Dirksen's daughter." Tactfully he glanced away from her look of stunned surprise and scanned the cloudless sky. "On rather short notice I've managed to squeeze in a few weeks' vacation. I asked Frances Forester to clear the place of scholars while I'm here."

Shane sucked in her breath. "So that's why everybody disappeared all at once."

He focused on her again, nodding, and suddenly her cheeks flooded with color. "But then why am *I* still here?"

"Because it seemed unfair to terminate your stay at this point." He got down from his horse. "Everyone else was working on a fairly flexible schedule that could accommodate delay. But Frances asked me to take special note of your case. According to the information she sent me, your Wanatoka research is necessary for you to complete a thesis in the near future."

"Before the end of June," Shane agreed numbly. "Without a master's degree, I won't be eligible for a teaching fellowship in the fall."

She didn't add that without the expected income from the fellowship, she wouldn't be able to meet the first payment on the sizable loan that had financed her graduate study. But in the moment of strained silence that followed, her panic was evident in her eyes.

Dirk Holland said a little more kindly, "It seemed apparent that if you, like the others, were requested to leave and return in six weeks, it might cause a hardship." His gaze leveled. "So I decided to let you stay on. Though I'll admit that in Hong Kong I pictured you as a studious, myopic male who'd always be tucked away in the library. It never occurred to me that Shane McBride was a woman."

Shane flushed. "Why didn't Miss Forester tell you?"

He mocked her gently. "Perhaps, like you, Miss Forester assumed that I keep tabs on the unusual names of actresses and well-known columnists. Or more to the point, I doubt if she ever gave it a thought. Sex"—he cleared his throat—"has never particularly interested Frances."

His dark-eyed glance traveled over Shane. "The question is academic, though, isn't it? Regardless of anyone's assumptions, you are quite definitely female."

Shane glared down at him. "Apparently because I *am* female I've been given second-rate treatment."

"Second-rate?" He scowled. "How do you figure that?"

She slid down off her horse, her annoyance increasing as she noted that at her full height she reached only to Dirk Holland's chin. "I was the only grant-holder left in the dark. All the *men* were informed."

"The men were involved. You weren't. My change of plans made no difference in yours. You're as free as you ever were to go ahead with whatever you're doing."

Indicating by the brusqueness of his tone that the discussion was at an end, he led the horses off to graze in a grassy spot at the edge of the woods. When he came back, Shane had plopped down on a large, flat rock and was surveying the ocean dejectedly.

He sat down beside her. "Are you still brooding?"

"Of course I am. No matter what you say, I know you want me to leave."

"Don't be silly. The matter is already settled."

"It isn't. You expected me to be a man. And now I'm an embarrassment to you because I'm a woman."

"I'm not in the least embarrassed."

"You are." Shane brought her head around. "Otherwise you wouldn't have mentioned your misunderstanding of the situation. In fact, there wouldn't have been a misunderstanding."

"I mentioned it because I think it's amusing."

"Then I think your amusement reveals a chauvinistic attitude! What difference does it make that I'm not the studious, myopic male whom you expected to lock himself away in the library?"

Dirk sighed. "It makes no difference at all."

But her agitation blocked out his reply. "It's quite clear now why you behaved as you did yesterday. You weren't jet-lagged. When you discovered you'd made a mistake, you shut yourself up to sulk in your room because a lone female in your house presented an awkwardness. You didn't know what to do about me."

His strong jaw turned to granite. "Since the minute I saw you astride that mare, I've known exactly what to do about you."

He reached out. The virile authority of his arms brought her up hard against his chest, making her a breathless captive. Then anger blazed through her with the suddenness of a hornet's sting.

She twisted free and on trembling legs leaped up to rail at him. "It won't work, Mr. Holland!"

"What won't work?" His gaze raked over her. "I'm merely behaving as a chauvinist is expected to."

"You're throwing your masculinity around to show me that I can't stay here, because if I do, I won't have a minute's peace."

"Is that what you think?" He grinned. "That I'll be after you all the time, trying to seduce you?"

"That's what you'd like me to think so you can get rid of me. Well, let me tell you something, Mr. Dirk Holland: I'm protected by the rules of the Dirksen Foundation. I signed an agreement and so did they."

A look of annoyance replaced his grin. "You don't need protection."

"You're darned right I don't. I can take care of myself, thank you." Her brown eyes snapped. "What I'm telling you is that you can't throw me off this island until the sixth day of May unless I agree to go, like those ninnies you've already sent packing. Or unless I fail in some way to follow the regulations governing my grant—and I have no intention of doing either one. You may own Wanatoka, sir, but you don't own me."

Dirk's dark eyes glittered. "Oh, for heaven's sake, knock the chip off your shoulder, will you?" He caught her hand and unceremoniously pulled her down again beside him. "Those 'ninnies,' as you've labeled five distinguished scientists, were well-compensated for their time. And as for you, I made up my mind in Hong Kong that you could stay. If I had wanted to renege on that decision, I'd have set Frances Forester on you yesterday." His tone softened. "By now you'd be back in Texas."

Shane swallowed. Those deep blue eyes. As irate as she was, she felt herself drowning in them. Her flesh still throbbed from his embrace, his hand holding hers was warm . . . caressing. . . . "It's extremely important for me to get this degree."

"I'm sure it is."

She caught the scent of his skin and felt a melting sensation deep inside her. She ought to run like crazy, she thought. But instead she heard herself say flatly, "If you're worried that I'll interfere with whatever you've planned for your vacation, I can assure you there isn't the slightest danger of that. If I stay, I shall take my meals in the kitchen. And I shall be very, very busy."

A slow smile lifted his lips. "Busy in the library?"

"Only part of the time." She drew herself up. "The subject of my thesis is the burial customs of North American Indians. I'm excavating a mound."

"Oh, I see. How delightful."

His sardonic response sparked her anger again. "It's odd, isn't it, how many fortunate people in this world own things they can't possibly appreciate, and others who could appreciate them never have a chance to."

"I believe you've had a chance," he answered coolly. "And thanks to my father's foresight, so have nearly two hundred other students over the past three years."

Shane's glare faded as she realized how perilously close to disaster her outburst had led her. Quickly she altered her tone. "You're right, of course. I beg your pardon. The Dirksen Foundation has been extremely generous."

"But not the Dirksen heir? Is that what you're thinking?"

Shane clamped her jaws together. Rising, she addressed him stiffly. "Mr. Holland, we seem to have gotten off to a very bad start. I'm sure your name appears in the information I received from the Foundation prior to coming here, and I apologize for not having recognized it when you introduced yourself."

He started up from the rock. "That isn't what I meant."

But Shane was determined to make her point. "I apologize also for seeming ungrateful, which I can assure you I am not. I realize fully how lucky I am to be here, particularly at a time that is so inconvenient for you. I do want to stay, however, and you can be sure I shall do my best to merit the trust you have placed in me."

When it was apparent that nothing more was to be offered from her tightly compressed lips, Dirk murmured with barely concealed amusement, "You're thoroughly steeped in academia, aren't you? Doesn't that artificial environment of the scholar bore you?"

She drew her lips into a thinner line. "I'm sure I don't know what you mean."

"You sounded just now as if you were quoting from a textbook. I liked you better when you were out there in the surf challenging my knowledge of teal loons." He took a step toward her, and she felt herself quiver in his towering shadow. "Lips as inviting as yours shouldn't spout cant."

Cheeks flaming, she wheeled about and stalked off toward her horse.

"Oh, and by the way," he called lazily after her, "if I were you, I'd forget about eating in the kitchen. That's Juno's territory. She'd never allow it."

Swinging herself into her saddle, Shane fumed in the knowledge that he was right. Juno, the cook, was a large, powerful woman whose proud, black eyes and commanding voice kept everyone stepping, even Frances Forester. Shane clenched her fist. Dirk Holland had her in a corner, and he knew it. She had no choice but to get along with him as best she could. But if he dared to make another pass at her, she vowed, she'd make sure that this was one vacation he'd be eager to see the end of.

Chapter Two

The burial mound Shane was excavating yielded nothing throughout the day, though she worked until nearly sundown sifting patiently through every grain of the sandy loam she had staked off that morning.

Was it possible that this was some other kind of mound? she wondered dejectedly, heading her Jeep back toward the mansion. If it were, that might account for the fact that none of the field notes left by her predecessors mentioned anything of interest on the northern end of the island.

Still feeling depressed and as inept as a first-year novice, she entered the house a quarter of an hour later and found Dirk Holland stretched out comfortably on the living-room sofa. Soft music floated from the tape deck and he held a drink in his hand.

"Will you come and join me?" he called when he caught sight of her hesitating in the hallway.

Shane longed to. When night fell, the island lost its springtime warmth and the fire's glow looked inviting. Holland himself looked inviting, she thought grudgingly. He was freshly shaved and had dressed for dinner in charcoal trousers and a champagne-colored corduroy jacket. He was leafing idly through a magazine, his feet on the coffee table, and his athletic leanness curved comfortably into the sofa cushions. Unbidden, a picture of herself rose in her mind, snuggled cozily against the wide wall of his chest, nestled beneath the shelter of his arm . . .

She turned away abruptly. "No, thank you. I'm on my way up for a bath."

He stopped her with a lazy warning. "You can save yourself the trouble. The water is shut off."

"What?" She wheeled around. "Why? What's happened?"

"Kimbo and his crew are laying a new line. With only you and me in the house, I decided this would be the best time to get the job done."

"Well, you might have told me!"

"I intended to mention it at breakfast, but you didn't show up."

She was always ravenous when she came in from riding, but this morning, rather than risk another encounter with him, she had made haste to get away while he was still at the stables. Now she was grimy from digging, her bones ached for a soak in a tub up to her neck, and he was offhandedly announcing that there wasn't any water! She felt childishly close to tears. "What do you expect me to do?"

"You're a graduate archaeologist, aren't you?"

His eyes glittered with challenge. "I imagine you've been on a dig or two where running water wasn't available."

She glared at his freshly shaven cheeks and clean shirt and knew that someone had drawn a tub for him. "On digs where there aren't bathing facilities I'm not expected to sit down at a formal dining table with the day's dirt still on me."

"Then I'll have Juno serve us in here." He took his feet down from the coffee table and brushed idly at its surface with his magazine. "Will that make you feel better?"

"A *bath* would make me feel better." Her eyes flashed angrily. "Obviously you've had one, so I shouldn't be too surprised if before the water was shut off, a tub was filled for me as well."

"That's a thought, isn't it?" His speculative gaze lingered on her scarlet face. "Go and see, why don't you? And I'll give you a rain check on the drink." With a brief nod of dismissal he went back to his reading.

Not only had Saphirra drawn a bath earlier, but she came at once when Shane rang, and added several kettles of steaming water to it from the supply that had been laid by for household use until Kimbo and his crew could finish up their work the following morning. Shane sank down to her chin in the recessed tub, luxuriating all the more because she had almost been denied the pleasure by her self-centered host. If she had listened to him, she wouldn't have known until she came up to bed that she could have bathed and dressed as usual for dinner. No doubt Dirk Holland would have considered that outcome a just retribution for her crack that morning about well-to-do persons like himself. She might have known he'd have to have the last word!

Then she realized she was smiling. Of course he had guessed how spoiled she had become, waited on hand and foot by Saphirra for the last ten days, fed excellent food, and given excellent wine to drink, to say nothing of the plush apartment she occupied all by herself.

Wrapping herself in a thick towel, she strolled to the door of the bathroom and looked out at the yellow-and-white loveliness of her bedroom. A small sitting room lay beyond, with a tea table and two Chippendale chairs set in a turreted alcove that looked out toward the Atlantic. She had never stayed in any place more charming. In fact, she had fallen in love with the whole house.

It was cavernous but cozy in a paradoxical way she hadn't been able to explain until one of the geologists commented that the place was built for comfort. That was it, of course. Everything was of the finest quality—draperies, furniture, parqueted floors—but all had the same warm, worn look as the coffee table Dirk had perched his feet on. Everything was meant to be used and enjoyed, and newcomers felt this at once and settled in as if it had always been home. Dirk would have guessed how quickly she had learned to take for granted all the niceties that were provided for her comfort, and he must have sat there waiting for her, relishing her shock when he made his announcement.

She confronted him loftily as soon as she came down again. "There's plenty of water."

"Is there indeed?" He cocked his head as if she had imparted a huge surprise. "That's welcome news."

He fixed his gaze on the pale-pink silk dress that clung to her graceful form. Her skin was tanned from long days at her dig, and the warm bath had brought a flattering glow to its smoothness. The fragrance of the floral perfume she had splashed on her wrists floated toward him. "I assume, then, that you're feeling refreshed?"

"Quite refreshed, thank you." Observing his admiring appraisal, Shane felt a disquieting sensation in her chest. "Your staff thinks of everything."

"They're not really my staff, you know." He got up and ambled to the oak sideboard. Without asking, he filled a goblet with sherry and brought it back to her. "Everyone who lives on the island owns stock in it. A percentage of any income derived from research funded by the Foundation goes back into its general fund for investment on the New York Stock Exchange. So whoever works in the house or on the grounds is actually working for himself."

Impressed by what he had said, Shane relaxed a little, but she still watched warily as he settled himself on the couch beside her. "That's rather a unique plan, isn't it?"

"It was Abraham's idea. My great-grandfather. He fell in love with the kindness of the people he found here. He admired their simple ways of doing things and their unassuming pride in Wanatoka. One of the first things he did after arriving here was use some of his capital to set up a corporation that was the basis for the current Dirksen Foundation. Then he invited the natives to earn shares of stock in return for whatever they could contribute toward building the house and cultivating small patches of a long-staple cotton that Abraham arranged to have shipped east to mills where fine shirt cloth was made.

"In recent years," he went on, "the cotton market has declined to the point where this isn't profitable. The cultivated acreage has gone back to woodlands, and the island work has pretty much narrowed down to maintaining the house and the grounds. But investments from those early days are still paying off, and some of the people you see now leading donkeys through the woods could treat themselves to new Cadillacs every year if they had any use for them."

Shane gazed at him, unaware of the becoming way her shining eyes lit up her face. "Your great-grandfather must have been a wonderful man."

"He's one of my heroes. My father was another." Unable to pull his glance away, Dirk stared frankly at the loveliness of her tawny skin. "After he inherited Wanatoka from his mother—Abraham's daughter—he was faced with a great many choices. Since he was the principal stockholder, he could have tripled his capital if he had sold. And there were times when he could have used the money, believe me. But he chose to vote with the islanders and hang on to Wanatoka. Just before his death they voted with him to set up the Foundation as it now exists."

"And you're carrying it on."

"In an advisory capacity primarily. My business concerns are mostly with Teletronics, Incorporated, the offshoot company of Abraham's interests in the telephone and the telegraph. My work carries me all over the world, so I have to leave the operation of the Foundation in other hands. But it's never far from my thoughts, no matter where I am."

Shane's cheeks burned as she recalled the things she had said on the beach. "I'm reminded that I ought to think before I 'spout cant,' as you so aptly put it this morning."

A faint smile played on his lips. "Don't feel too badly. I have an idea you were just evening the score with the grouch you'd given a ride to the day before. Anyway, you weren't privy to what I've just told you when we were disagreeing."

Shane gazed thoughtfully at him. Was it possible that he wasn't the arrogant egotist she had supposed him to be? Saphirra's protective attitude toward him seemed to confirm that, as did the fact that out of consideration for the degree she was trying to earn, he had allowed her to stay on. It was obvious to her now that his return to the island was a private kind of rendezvous with his past that he couldn't have welcomed sharing with a stranger, and she warmed toward him even more.

"How often do you get back to Wanatoka?"

He rose and filled his glass again. "I try to make it every six months or so, but things have been hectic recently."

She thought of what he had said about the chess game in Hong Kong. Even the rich had their troubles, she supposed.

"It's been a year since I was here last," he went on. "I had no idea I'd get to come this time until unexpectedly a snarl untangled itself." He leaned against the hearthstones, and she saw for the first time that lines of fatigue were still etched around his eyes. "Ordinarily I try to plan ahead when I'm coming so that no one who is awarded a grant for that period will be inconvenienced. It makes for a much smoother operation when one doesn't have to interrupt serious work."

Shane dropped her gaze and toyed with the stem of her wineglass. "I got the impression this morning that you don't hold the excavation of the burial mounds in very high regard."

"Not at all." His low laughter brought her eyes back up. "If I gave you that impression," he said, "it's because I was feeling chauvinistic again." The corners of his mouth twitched. "You see, you don't at all fit my picture of a female archaeologist."

"Really?" She tried to keep her voice even, but each time his gaze moved over her and the topic turned personal, she found it harder to breathe. "And what is that picture, if I may ask?"

"You ought to be forty at least," he answered. "You ought to wear great, clumping boots all the time and have frizzy red hair. And you ought to have a long, pointed nose to sniff out treasures."

Shane laughed in spite of her annoyance. "That's an outmoded view if I ever heard one."

"It is." His gaze fastened on the parting of her pink lips. "And here's another," he said softly, moving toward her. "A woman as beautiful as you should perhaps think twice about spending time alone on an island with a man who can't stop looking at her."

Shane's heart seemed to stop beating. "Is that a warning?"

"I think it could be construed as one."

She forced herself to return his gaze. "We aren't alone. According to the Foundation brochures, Wanatoka boasts a population of forty-two men, women, and children." She moistened her lips. "Some of whom are in the kitchen right now."

His stare turned luminous. "And they won't come out until I let them know we're ready for dinner."

She managed a cool smile. "Dinner is served promptly at eight. According to the clock on the mantel, you have exactly three minutes to make your move."

"When I'm on the island," he answered with quiet assurance, "dinner is served whenever I want it."

"You're contradicting yourself, you know." She pulled in her breath, wondering if he had noticed how her wineglass trembled when she set it down. "This morning you told me I'd be silly to leave. Now you're warning me that I ought to."

His gaze traveled with heart-stopping slowness from her lips to the soft curves of silk that covered her breasts. "This morning you were wearing a faded green shirt and blue jeans."

She got to her feet. "You *are* a chauvinist."

"I'm a man who reacts in a positive way to a beautiful woman."

"Every time you see one?" Her heart had begun to beat unreliably. "No wonder you're always so busy."

But the taunt was lost on him. He took a step forward and gravely, deliberately pulled her into his arms.

Automatically she resisted, curling her small hands into fists against the muscular swell that his coat sleeves concealed. But almost at once her flesh betrayed her, yielding itself with quivering eagerness to the power of his embrace.

A glorious warmth radiated from his body. It spread as his mouth touched her skin, her cheeks first, and then her lips, turning moistly on them. Pulling her closer, he fitted her to him. A tremor of excitement shot through her as a craving she had not known herself capable of engulfed her with a fiery urgency.

One of his hands whispered over the silk that shaped her waist and slid down to settle provocatively on the curve of her hip. The kiss deepened, and she felt herself swirling suddenly through dark waters, out of her depth, helpless while restraint wriggled away, eluding her will as slickly as an eel.

But in another moment desire became paramount, honing itself to a fine, biting edge as he pressed her against the hard planes of his body. Breathing his maleness, she leaned into the wall of his chest and gave herself over to the union of their mouths and to the sheer ecstasy of being bound up in his embrace.

Then, through the heated haze surrounding them, the clock struck. Shane opened her eyes and the room came back into focus. Dirk stepped back, watching with glowing eyes as Shane's hand flew up to her hair and then fluttered back down to straigthen the collar where his lean, curling fingers had caressed her throat.

Unnerved by his scrutiny, she worked desperately to calm her thoughts. In Dirk's embrace her emotions had dictated her behavior, overruling every other priority, dismissing without ceremony all previous notions about the kind of man she might fall in love with . . . and when . . . and where.

Determined to reestablish herself on firm ground, she lashed out at him in a caustic tone that belied her emotional state. "All right, Mr. Holland, you've made your point. Let me make mine. I'm flattered, of course, that you find me attractive—"

The midnight blue of his eyes deepened. "Attractive is a rather inadequate word."

She brought her chin up to combat the smile that tugged at his lips. "I don't deny either that your attractiveness has a certain appeal for me as well. An advantage," she pointed out tightly, "that you obviously enjoy exploiting. But I would remind you that my reason for coming to Wanatoka is a serious one. I have time only for my work. A repetition of what just happened here would not be at all welcome."

Encouraged by his silence, she added with more confidence, "Fortunately we are both mature, civilized adults, and I'm sure I can count on you to have enough respect for the Foundation your father created not to sully it by imposing yourself on one of its endowed scholars."

He stayed quiet for a moment longer, studying her with his dark, dancing eyes. Finally he said in a low voice that shook her to the core, "You're right, of course. I would never impose myself. When the time comes for us to make love, you'll want it as much as I do."

Reaching around her, he pulled a brocaded cord that hung against the wall. "Now I suggest that as mature adults we adjourn to the dining room to enjoy the civlized dinner Juno has prepared for us."

Chapter Three

The dinner Shane and Dirk Holland shared was, in her opinion, anything but civilized. Certainly it was one she would never forget. Although he was a perfect gentleman, pulling out her chair and paying strict attention to all the finer points of etiquette, every look he gave her, every softly spoken word was loaded with sensuous overtones. Every glance seemed to undress her. Passing her a dish of baked oysters, he closed his hand for an instant over hers, and beneath its subtle pressure she felt her flesh ignite.

He kept the conversation on harmless topics, but even when he was in the midst of discussing the history of the telegraph system in the United States, his gaze dipped brazenly into the open throat of her dress and lingered there until her hand nervously brought the cloth together. By the time dessert was finally served, the pink silk was clinging to her moist skin and she felt as aroused as if he had been kissing her passionately for the past half-hour instead of quietly partaking of Juno's fine food.

* * *

Shane hardly slept that night, dreading the inevitable encounters morning would bring. But in the days that followed, she saw little of Dirk Holland. Though she rode down to the surf each dawn, he did not join her again. He seldom appeared at the appointed hours for breakfast or lunch, and in the evening when they met for dinner, he treated her in the same cool, impersonal manner with which he might confront an utter stranger.

At first she felt only relief. There was to be no repetition of Dirk's kiss or of that trying dinner. He had played his little joke, and that was the end of it. Gratefully she tended to her studies, which demanded more and more of her time because of the disappointing burial mound of the north shore. She had counted on a discovery of her own to serve as the ultimate focus for her thesis. Wanatoka, she had been told, always yielded interesting artifacts. But now it seemed that she was going to have to make do with secondhand field notes left in the library by her predecessors. Depressed but diligent, she pored over them while the island came alive with spring.

The long, uninterrupted hours at her books soon began to wear on her nerves. Feelings of restlessness made concentration all but impossible. Then Dirk's face began appearing on the pages of her notes. His blue eyes stared up at her, smokily reflecting her own desire. Sometimes without absorbing a single word she was reading, she turned pages, recalling in minute detail the kiss they had shared, or their morning ride together in the sparkling surf.

Frustrated, she went for long walks, torn between the hope of seeing him and the dread of having it actually happen. But if she caught sight of him at all, he was usually with Kimbo and his crew, inspecting something or engaging in manual labor with the natives. His idea of a vacation seemed to be to exhaust himself physically. Apparently the work agreed with him, however, for whenever she did catch a glimpse of him, bare-chested and bronzed, the powerful swell of his shoulders and arms affirmed that he was a male in peak condition.

Several torturous days passed, and she gave up trying to pretend that the only thing of importance to her was the degree she had set out to earn. Whether she liked it or not, Dirk had taken over her life. His kiss had so thoroughly shaken her up that just gazing at him through the underbrush stirred feelings in her that she had never experienced—restless, erotic feelings that provoked embarrassingly sexual images that even invaded her dreams. Shane flushed whenever she thought of how eagerly she had begun to look forward to those nocturnal encounters, as elusive as they were.

Sometimes in them Dirk materialized suddenly out of a mist and swept her into his arms, bringing his lips within inches of hers, but never quite kissing her. Sometimes he lay down beside her, stroking her bare breasts, gazing with hot longing at their taut nipples, but never bringing his lips to them as she yearned for him to do.

When she awoke to the morning shadows of her yellow-and-white room, she felt lonely and torn. The sane, logical pattern she had laid out for her life had broken apart. She still held all the pieces, but every day it was harder to believe that they would ever fit together again.

One morning, passing through a stand of holly on one of her walks, she caught sight of Dirk in a clearing ahead, naked to the waist, sawing a pine log with the help of a young black worker. His tanned skin glistened wetly, and as she paused, hidden from view among the spiked leaves, she felt the tension of his swaying torso insinuating itself into her own bodily rhythms. Her heart hammered. Drops of moisture popped out above her lip and erotic prickles swarmed up her spine.

When at last the saw cut through and the log dropped in two even lengths, Dirk straightened. His gaze drifted, resting briefly on the emerald leaves that shielded her, and for a moment she felt herself standing bare-fleshed before him. Her knees shook and her breath rasped raggedly in her throat as desire welled up in her.

That night at the dinner table, she could hardly meet Dirk's gaze. But fortunately, for the first time, company shared their meal.

Frances Forester, her stocky form outfitted

neatly in a twill suit and faultless white blouse, appeared in the foyer just as Shane was coming down the stairs. Dirk joined them and they all went into the dining room together.

Ordinarily Dirk sat at the head of the table and Shane sat on his right, but this evening for some obscure reason he gave the host's place to Frances and seated himself opposite Shane.

The first time she met his stare head-on, blood flooded her cheeks. She recalled her erotic experience in the holly thicket and thought for a minute she might faint with the crush of embarrassment and unrelenting desire that bore down on her.

But Dirk shifted his attention to Frances, and after that, Shane took care to glance at him only when there was no avoiding it. Otherwise, all she could see was his broad brown chest and its curling mass of glistening hair, as if the blue cotton shirt he wore beneath his jacket were as transparent as rain.

To Shane's great relief, Frances Forester was never at a loss for words. The Center's middle-aged director had an opinion about everything, and for a time neither she nor Dirk appeared to notice how quiet Shane was.

Then suddenly during dessert—a fresh-fruit concoction that was one of Juno's specialties— the older woman turned her hawkish gaze directly toward Shane.

"How is your work progressing, McBride?"

Shane caught the flicker of amusement in

Dirk's eyes and glanced away quickly. "Very well, thank you, Miss Forester. Although I'm afraid I'm not uncovering anything startling at my dig."

The woman peered at her. "For heaven's sakes, why not?"

Shane shrank from admitting that she still wasn't sure what she was excavating. "Actually I haven't spent much time at it lately. I've had other things to do." Her voice trailed away as she reached for her water glass. "Research is occupying most of my time."

Frances Forester frowned in obvious disapproval. "To reach a goal," she intoned, "one must openly pursue."

"Yes, indeed," Dirk echoed, as solemn as an owl. "There's nothing that pays off like dedicated, open pursuit." He shot a wicked glance at Shane. "Is there, McBride?"

Her heart stopped. Did that mean he had seen her ogling him from the holly? She felt like sinking through the floor. He might have observed her at other times too, on her solitary walks, and guessed how much she longed for his company. She glared across the table at him. Devil! He'd probably made himself scarce for that very reason.

After that, everything he said seemed to Shane to have a double meaning. When Frances Forester finally put down her coffeecup in the living room and rose to say good night, Shane was so keyed up she jumped when Dirk suggested that the two of them walk Frances back to her quarters.

"There's a full moon," he added.

On the point of refusing him, Shane read the challenge in his smile and gritted her teeth. "A full moon? Then I'd love to come."

Going over, the three of them walked single-file down the moonlit path that led through the live oaks to Frances' cottage. But when they were nearly there, the path widened and Frances mentioned casually that along a similar walkway one of Kimbo's men had come upon a seven-foot diamond-back rattlesnake earlier in the day. "One must watch one's step," she said crisply, "now that we know there are serpents abroad."

Dirk made a snickering sound, but Shane's heart pumped. Rattlers were not a rarity where she came from, but she had never encountered one seven feet long. "They don't come out at night, do they?"

"Indeed they do," Frances asserted. "The ground is cooler then, you see."

Dirk contradicted her brusquely, "In April they aren't seeking cool ground, Frances. They're barely out of hibernation." He slipped a protective arm around Shane's waist as she shied away from a fallen limb at the edge of the path. "It's summer nights that bring out snakes."

"That's true, I suppose." Frances opened her front door and flicked on a light. "But one can never be too cautious. Well, good night, you two. I enjoyed the evening." She directed one of her rare smiles at Shane. "You must come over and dine with me soon. Rabbit stew is my specialty. Dirk can tell you how delicious it is."

"Frances Forester is an interesting woman," Shane commented dryly when she and Dirk were on their way back to the mansion. "Just when you think you've figured her out to be a cold fish, she turns out to be all warm and human."

"She was my father's secretary for years," Dirk answered. "She still sees me as a kid in short pants who has to be warned about stepping on snakes."

The chagrin in his voice made Shane relax her guard a little. "I thought the warning was for me."

His arm brushed against hers. "Well, perhaps it was for both of us. Anyway, her heart's in the right place, even though at times she behaves like a snapping turtle."

Shane tensed again at his touch. The moonlight washing over the angles of his face stirred up a tightness in her chest that made it hard to breathe. Her dreams of him rose vividly in her mind. Nervously she inquired, "When you were a boy, did you spend much time here?"

"Not nearly as much as I wanted to." They came out onto the open lawn. "I was usually here in the summer, but the rest of the year my father packed me off to school in the East."

"You sound as if your mother might not have approved."

A muscle tightened in his jaw. "My mother was no longer living here then."

"Oh. I'm sorry. Do you have brothers and sisters?" Shane asked hurriedly.

"I have an older sister."

With a sinking feeling she saw that he was guiding her toward the end of the porch where there was a swing.

Casually he asked, "Will you be too cool if we sit out for a while?"

Shane shivered, more from panic than from the chilly night air. This was the moment she had longed for. But now she dreaded it because she was meeting it with her mind still in turmoil. What did she want? To stick with her plan to remain independent and objective in all her relationships until she was firmly established with her teaching fellowship? Or did she want to give in to this insane craving that was upsetting all her days, to entangle herself emotionally and risk spreading herself so thin she might never finish her thesis?

While she hesitated, Dirk took her hand in his and led her to the swing. Shane sank down, snuggling deeper into her sweater. Out of the air she plucked the first thing she could think of that might divert him. "Where does your sister live?"

"Indigo?" He kept hold of her hand, examining with his thumb the delicate ovals of her fingertips. "She lives in Switzerland. Her husband is an international banker."

"Indigo," Shane repeated. There was something reassuring in that beautiful, old-fashioned name.

"It's the color of her eyes," Dirk said.

"Of yours too," Shane answered without thinking.

They sat still, looking at each other for an instant. Then Dirk said, "Our black nurse named her. One of the first crops the Wanatoka slaves raised for their owners was indigo. It flourished, and they reaped the benefits of the dye market. When that same deep blue showed up in my sister's eyes, the natives, all of them descendants of those original slaves, regarded it as a good omen." He chuckled softly. "Then I came along and they wanted to name me Indigo Baas, just for good measure. Thank heaven my father wouldn't hear of it."

"Oh, I don't know." Shane found it impossible to stifle the surge of joy his nearness produced in her. "It has a certain ring. I. B. Holland," she teased, "I like it. Don't you?"

"No, I don't." Then all at once he bent and brought his lips to hers, at the same time gathering her into his arms with a sureness and strength that felt so right she clung to him, forgetting everything except the rapture washing over her as his mouth turned on hers.

But her thoughts cleared in an instant, and she recalled the gauntlet he had flung down on that memorable evening when his eyes had seduced her at the dinner table. The truth came crashing in on her. She did want him to make love to her.

She had been aching all week to be crushed against his body. But he was taking too much for granted, blatantly ignoring every point she had made to him that evening about the kind of behavior she expected from Abraham Dirksen's great-grandson. If she admitted now how deeply she desired him, the rules they played by would be his alone.

Wriggling free of his embrace, she blurted out tightly, "Why do you always have to spoil things?"

His heated gaze stayed on her. "Do I?"

"You complicate them, to say the least."

"We can handle complications, can't we?" His dark eyes glinted in the moonlight. "After all, we're two mature, civilized adults."

"You enjoy making fun of me, don't you?"

"I enjoy kissing you more." He shifted, pulling her over against the tautness of his body. He brought his mouth to hers again, kissing her with an urgent, tantalizing force that deepened slowly. His tongue, parting her lips, explored the dark, sweet softness of her mouth and played disastrously against her will to resist, but she managed a choked protest. "Please—don't."

He came back thickly, "Why not?"

"Necking in a porch swing," she answered in a strangled voice. "That's adolescent."

"Adolescent?" Suddenly his body hardened. His mouth drove into hers, purposeful, plunging, thoroughly the kiss of a full-fledged man. When at last he took his lips away, she throbbed in every nerve center. Her raw senses ached for him.

"Let's go inside," he whispered thickly.

The muscular swells of his torso pressed against her. The lower part of his body, angled along her thighs, left no doubt as to how far advanced his passion was. Her own desire equaled his, but she managed to say through a constricted throat, "Yes, let's do go inside. We can say good night and forget that this evening ever happened."

"We can go upstairs and go to bed together." He tightened his embrace. "And don't pretend that you don't want to."

"I don't. And I'm not pretending."

"Then you're lying." His lips moved down to the hollow of her throat and on to the valley between her breasts.

She dug her nails into his neck. "Let me go!"

All at once he did, sitting back, watching with glittering eyes while she grabbed at her sweater and bunched it tightly at her throat. "You ought to be ashamed of yourself," she said harshly.

"I am." He eyed her with steely reserve. "I should have had you halfway up the stairs by now."

"You make me sick."

"That can happen too. Repressed desire. It acts like a poison."

Shane sprang up from the swing. "First thing in the morning, I intend to speak to Frances Forester."

"What will you say, Shane?" His long body uncoiled and he took hold of her again. "Will you tell her that I was sexually abusive? Was I? Or was I only responding the way any man would to the signals you've been sending me for days?"

"What a preposterous thing to say!"

His hot gaze raked her. "I read you, my dear, like an open book. Those averted glances every evening at dinner. Moist palms when I hand you a sherry. On the beach the day I came, you were as open and friendly as a morning glory. Now you're tied in knots whenever we meet." He drew her up against him. "Have I penetrated your dreams yet?" His chest rose and fell heavily. "Yes—I can see I have. Except that there's a glass wall between us, isn't there? What you want, you can see. But you can't have it. So near and yet so far."

"You collosal egotist! Do you think all I have to do is think about you?"

His even gaze riveted her. "If it can happen to me, it can happen to you."

Her breath left her. "What? What did you say?"

He muttered hotly against her cheek. "Do you think I've been tearing this island apart and putting it back together every day just for the fun of it?"

She answered faintly, "I haven't thought about it, one way or the other."

His low laughter scalded her neck. "That's

another lie. Kiss me, Shane, the way you want to, with all stops out and no holds barred."

But still the hard core of her independence resisted him. "No—"

"Then I'll kiss you." His shadow merged with hers into a single pulsating column. The fierce demand of his mouth parted her lips. One hand clamped possessively at the nape of her neck, the other skillfully, erotically kneaded her breast.

Inside of Shane the flames he sparked raged out of control. Her whole being cried out for him except the one defensive corner of her brain where the temperature stayed at zero. There are serpents abroad, Frances Forester's prim voice reminded her. And in Dirk's ardent kiss Shane sensed all at once that a part of him was holding back, too. He brimmed over with passion, but still he wasn't involved totally.

When he took his mouth away, she gasped out, "Stop—"

'More, did you say?" he murmured thickly, and brought it down again. Knowingly, selectively, he went about his nibbling, persistent torture while she felt herself sinking again under the powerful thrust of his appeal. He kissed her eyelids, her throat, her temples, and she melted at the moist roving of his lips. The tip of his tongue trailed the intricate whorls of her ear. He came back to her mouth, and this time he found it supple and loosened with passion, hungry for his. He took it, her response triggering moans from deep inside his heaving chest.

Suddenly Shane realized that her hands were independently exploring his body, pressuring his narrow hips, feverishly stroking his chest. But she was torn between intense desire that teetered on the brink of fulfillment and a stubborn refusal to let go of the last shred of independence that had made her stand up to him before. He seemed to feel her tense and stiffen.

The harsh rasp of his breath protested, "Let yourself go, Shane. Don't you know how special this moment can be?"

"I don't want to know!" In a swift, whirling motion she pulled away, peeling his unwilling fingers from her waist and standing back, tugging at her sweater.

His eyes burned in the moonlight. "Coward." The bitter undertones bruised her ears. "You want all the thrills of the roller coaster without taking the ride."

"That's cruel and unfeeling."

"You should know. You're the expert." With both hands he smoothed back his tousled hair. Then he strode past her, letting the front door close with a decisive bang.

Chapter Four

The next morning Shane waited at the breakfast table until Dirk appeared. Freshly shaven and clad in his usual jeans, this time with a checkered shirt tucked into them, he stared at her and then muttered a curt good morning.

"You're late, aren't you?" he said.

Shane stared back at him. "No. You are."

"I didn't sleep well."

"Neither did I."

Their glances locked in the tensely charged air. Then Dirk moved to the buffet and filled his plate. When he came back and sat down, he took a long time buttering his toast.

Finally, without looking up, he said, "All right, so I owe you an apology. Last night was a mistake. If you want to see Frances Forester, I'll make the appointment for you myself. Is there anything else I can do to smooth your ruffled feathers?"

Shane's nostrils flared. The red of her shirt seemed to flow up her throat to stain her cheeks. "I am not a fidgety little hen."

He raised his eyes slowly, and for an instant a shadow of laughter passed over his lips. "You could have fooled me out there on the porch."

"You're not adding much to the credibility of your apology."

"Then I apologize for that too."

"In other words, what you're saying is that you'd like me just to leave you alone."

"That's right." He dug into the marmalade jar. "Give the lady a brass ring for hitting the bull's-eye."

"A black eye is what I'd like to give you."

Dirk put down his knife. "Did I ask you to hang around here and spoil my breakfast? Wasn't last night enough to satisfy your sadistic nature?"

But when he saw her push her chair back, he put out a conciliatory hand. "Oh, here—wait a minute." He clasped her gently around the wrist. "If we have to inflict pain on each other, let's at least fortify ourselves first."

She pulled her hand free. "I've eaten, thank you."

"Then how about giving me a chance?" His look softened as he filled her coffeecup. "Don't be so upset. Nothing so terrible has happened. Our timing was off, that's all."

She waited a moment, trying to get her voice under control. "Timing or whatever, I can't possibly stay on here. You know that, don't you?"

"No, I don't know that." A half-smile twisted the lips she was longing against all reason to kiss.

"Consider my point of view. Do you imagine I'd risk putting my head in the lion's mouth twice? After last night," he concluded dryly, "you're as safe here as if twenty chaperones were looking after you."

Shane winced and thought achingly of how little he knew. She'd never be safe with him again because out there on that chilly porch he had branded her with his kisses. Her body believed it belonged to him, and no matter what the cool, independent part of her brain said, her heart went on yearning for his touch. Even here at this bright, sunny breakfast table, all that was female within her was longing for darkness and shadows . . . for his arms around her, for his hard body to invite her again into his bed.

The thoughts that had kept her awake last night had shattered her self-confidence. She didn't know this woman who was obsessed by physical sensations and erotic imaginings. The Shane McBride whose carefully ordered life plan provided for a conventional courtship—candy and flowers, a ring, and no more than a few mild, intimate fumblings before the trip to the altar—that Shane who had believed herself totally in control of her emotions had vanished into thin air. The passionate woman who had taken her place couldn't be relied on to behave for even five minutes if she ever had another opportunity to make love with the indigo-eyed male brooding at her from across the table.

Involuntarily, she sighed.

"What a heartfelt sound," Dirk commented mildly. He rested his chin on the heel of his hand. "Are you grieving over that burial mound you'll have to leave behind?"

The remark was so ridiculously inappropriate and so far from what she was actually thinking that a smile forced itself onto Shane's lips. At once she felt better, particularly when Dirk smiled back at her. She loved the way his craggy face cracked open. She loved the laugh lines around his eyes and the creases around his mouth. Her heart began to thud, but she picked up on the tone he had set with his lighthearted teasing.

"I don't think it's a burial mound at all," she said. "I think it's a prehistoric ants' nest."

He leaned back and laughed out loud.

The sound filled the room and Shane felt a further lightening of her mood as she continued. "I thought I'd made such a great discovery because none of the field notes in the library even mention it. But the reason they don't, I've decided, must be because it doesn't amount to anything."

"I'm sorry." His expression sobered. "That leaves quite a gaping hole in your research, I'd imagine."

"It does, yes. But it doesn't matter," she added quickly. The last thing she needed at this point was to have him feel sorry for her. "I'll finish my thesis anyway. When I set a goal for myself, I always reach it, no matter what."

One of his dark brows quirked upward skeptically. "Is that so?"

Shane flushed, realizing how conceited she must sound. "It's a fault actually. A compunction to overachieve that's probably a little childish, in this instance particularly." How idiotic to lay herself open to further scorn! But with Dirk's speculative stare upon her, she felt compelled to go on. "I'll get my degree because I've made up my mind I will and because it's imperative that I teach." She paused. "But I'm not really a dedicated scholar."

Her heartbeat quickened at his look of surprise. "I'm just a very curious individual," she continued, somewhat defensively. "I got into archaeology because I'm fascinated by lives that were lived hundreds of years ago. Whenever I come across a potsherd or an arrowhead or the remains of a campsite, my imagination works overtime. I can't wait to put the whole thing together, like the pieces of a jigsaw puzzle. But primarily it's the romance of the dig that appeals to me. I'm bored senseless by statistics. I find them drier than the bones I dig up, and when the time comes to deal with them, I want to bow out and leave all that tedious drudgery to someone else."

It was the most revealing speech she'd ever made to him, and it left her breathless and pink-cheeked and more than a little unnerved. She sipped from the coffeecup he had filled for her, and tried to regain her composure.

"I suppose you think that's awful. For me to have come here masquerading as a scholar when dozens of real scholars would give their eyeteeth to be in my place."

"Let them worry about themselves." But his blue eyes probed hers in a way that made her heart sink. Who could blame him for despising her even more now, for misrepresenting herself in a second way? She had no choice now but to leave, and of course she'd never see him again. Their paths would never cross in the real world. It was only Wanatoka—the island time had forgotten—that had enabled them to meet at all.

"Where is this mound of yours?" he asked.

"On the northern tip of the island." Oh, those blue eyes, she mourned. This morning there were little flecks of silver in them. She recalled his embrace, his hands moving with the certainty of possession over her body . . .

"It's right in the middle of a strangely bare strip of ground. That was what attracted me in the first place. There's such lush growth on all the other parts of the island."

"It's strangely bare," he told her in a tone of authority, "because last fall a low-grade hurricane spawned tornadic winds over that portion of the island. The twister dipping down denuded it. Before that, the vegetation was so dense no one bothered trying to penetrate it."

Shane's eyes opened wide. "Then of course there's no mention of my mound in the library—no one ever saw it before!" She sat up on the edge of her chair. "Maybe there's something there after all."

"It certainly seems worth looking into." He grinned suddenly, pleased with his pun, but Shane failed to notice.

"It's true that my excavations have been fairly shallow. In sandy loam the Indians might have found it necessary to bury deeper—"

Then all at once her excitement faded. She slumped back in her chair. "I'll make a note of that for future archaeologists who come to Wanatoka."

Dirk gazed at her keenly. "And let them take all the credit for your discovery?"

"I haven't discovered anything yet."

"Then let's go do something about that."

"Now? We can't. I'm leaving." She pushed back from the table and he saw for the first time that her red blouse was tucked into a beige suit skirt. Picking up her jacket and purse from the chair beside her, she lowered her gaze. "I've left a letter for Frances Forester. I've resigned my grant. I'm taking the mail boat out this morning."

Dirk got to his feet. "You can't do that." At Shane's startled look he added gruffly, "You'll be seasick again if you take the mail boat." With elaborate concentration he fitted the top back on the marmalade jar. "I'll signal the mainland for a plane, but you'll have to allow time for it to get here."

Shane's heart sank. Time had become her

enemy. It took only a moment for two pairs of lips to meet.

"While you're waiting," Dirk said casually, "you'll have a chance to take another look at your ants' nest." He focused directly on her troubled face. "You'd never forgive yourself if it turned out to be something spectacular that you could have been in on from the first."

Would she ever forgive herself if she stayed on? Shane wondered. The chemistry between them was too explosively sexual. Each time he touched her the possibility that she could resist him became more remote. Never before had she desired a man so intensely that everything else she valued was pushed into the background. To be so out of control of her own emotions was upsetting enough, but as Dirk had pointed out, if she walked away now from this intriguing development at her dig, the curiosity that had first drawn her to archaeology would nip at her heels forever.

Sensing her dilemma, Dirk moved swiftly to take advantage of it. "We'll spend the day at the excavation site. With both of us working we ought to turn up something if there's anything there. If there isn't, what have you lost?"

He strode purposefully toward the kitchen door and called out a crisp command. "Juno, send somebody out to fetch the Jeep, please. I'll need lunch for two right away. Something hearty, and put in a bottle of wine."

Lisa St. John

Upstairs, changing her clothes, Shane quivered, thinking of how she had allowed Dirk to take charge. She knew why. Deep down, she wanted to stay more than she wanted to go. The mature, civilized side of her that he enjoyed ridiculing had dressed that morning for travel, but in her heart of hearts she wanted to remain on Wanatoka, or else she would have left a letter for Dirk as well as for Frances Forester and not waited at the breakfast table for him.

Facing up to her true feelings helped to settle the uncertainty muddying her thoughts, just as confessing to Dirk that the childishness of rigidly adhering to goals she set for herself had enabled her for the first time to admit it to herself. If so much of her wanted to stay here with Dirk, no matter what the consequences, could it be a mistake to do so?

She had never let a man's physical appeal count for more than qualities of mind and heart. But she had never met a man like Dirk Holland before. Besides, she comforted herself as she went down the stairs, when had she ever given him a chance to show her what kind of person he was? They were always quarreling. She was always finding fault with him. Going back to the dig was probably a pointless waste of time, but at least it might give them an opportunity to learn to know each other in a setting that wasn't fraught with sexual overtones.

But when she came out onto the veranda and saw him leaning against the Jeep, his tanned legs bare below the khaki shorts he wore and the lines of his wide, muscular chest outlined by a soft knit shirt, she felt her knees tremble. Climbing in beside him, she prayed silently for so much archaeological excitement at the burial mound that the excitement he had already aroused in her simply by brushing her hand when he opened the door for her, would pale into insignificance.

In only a few hours her wish came astonishingly close to coming true.

Chapter Five

❧

By eleven o'clock, the day had turned hot and sultry. Sand and grit stuck to Shane's skin, and the back of Dirk's shirt was dark with sweat. Working side by side, they had sifted through six inches of loam in an area two feet square, and they had uncovered nothing but a half-dozen odd little pottery chips that Dirk jokingly called petrified ants. Their strange shapes nagged at something in Shane's memory, but it was too remote to recall, particularly when every few minutes she came into contact with some part of Dirk—his strong brown hands as he passed over more loam for her to examine, or his knee brushing hers. . . . Equally unsettling was the way he seemed to forget for long moments that she was there. But as soon as she managed to forget him for an instant, his dark-eyed gaze returned and bored into her.

Worn out at last with the whole unrewarding morning, she moved away to sink down in the shade of the only oak that had withstood the tornado's winds. "We're spinning our wheels," she muttered as Dirk joined her. "Let's break for lunch."

"Lunch?" he chided. "You just finished breakfast."

"*You* just finished breakfast," she countered, poking irritably at the earth around the tree's trunk. "I was through half an hour before you ever appeared."

His indigo eyes twinkled. "And while you sat there fuming, you burned up all your energy, is that it?"

Grinning, he lifted the lid of the picnic basket. As soon as they had set out in the Jeep, the unpleasantness of the evening before had seemed to melt from his memory.

Now, he said amiably, "Okay, let's see what we have here for a starving archaeologist." He began hauling things out and laying them on the cloth Juno had provided. "Boiled ham on biscuit sandwiches, a nice cool bottle of Chardonnay. And for dessert—"

Shane's excited voice cut him off. "Dirk—look at this!"

"What is it?"

She held out a small metal object she had pulled out of the sand. "A medallion. Spanish!" With trembling fingers she handed it to him. "Look at the lettering. And there's a Madonna in the middle."

Dirk rubbed the gray disc on his jeans. Time had darkened it and crusts of mineral deposits had defaced one side, but undeniably it was a religious emblem of some sort.

Tense with excitement, Shane leaned closer. "At some time in the past there must have been a Spanish settlement here."

Dirk said cautiously, "There's no record of one."

"This is the record!"

"This is only a single artifact." His gaze warmed sympathetically. "Can you draw that kind of conclusion from one small medal? How do you know it wasn't dropped by a traveling priest or a soldier on reconnaissance?"

"Because it's not the only proof I have." She darted back to the digging site and returned in a moment with the pottery shards Dirk had labeled petrified ants.

"Everything clicked when I saw that medal. I recognize these now." She dropped down beside him, so close their foreheads touched. "They're parts of shroud clasps. If we keep on digging, Dirk, we'll find what the shrouds enclosed—and heaven knows what else! This may be an Indian burial mound, but there were Spaniards here too. I'll stake my degree on it."

Still not convinced, Dirk reminded her, "All the Spanish settlements were farther down the coast, nearer Florida."

"All the *known* settlements were. That's what makes this such a fabulous find." She sat back on her heels, her eyes sparkling. "I have the proof right here in my hands that what historians have believed for decades is wrong."

"Wait a minute," Dirk cautioned. "Before you electrify the world with an announcement, let's see what else we can uncover."

But her enthusiasm was too contagious to withstand, and Dirk was as eager as she was to get started. While he cleared the area, Shane gathered the tools for digging and arranged them like a surgeon's instruments in a circle around the tree. Then they set to work.

In an hour's time they had sifted out of the loose loam half a dozen ruby-red rosary beads and at last, to the astonishment of them both, an ancient saddle ornament.

Admiration filled Dirk's voice as he gazed down at the silver-plated relic at their feet. "This means there were horses, doesn't it?"

He grabbed for Shane, giving her an exuberant hug. "You bright little wizard! There really *was* a permanent settlement here—and you've uncovered it."

"We've uncovered it." Shane wrapped her arms around him, thinking only of the thrill of discovery they were sharing. In a giddy kiss of triumph her lips met his.

Then, all at once, suppressed desire took over, ripping through them with the swiftness of a prairie fire.

"Shane—"

Spanish relics forgotten, Dirk's arms tightened about her. They clung to each other, aware only of an overwhelming need for nearness, for exploring the passion that shook them. Dirk's mouth settled hungrily on Shane's parted lips. She threw her head back and breathed in his aroma, musky and sun-kissed.

He told her thickly, "You might have gone away this morning."

She murmured dissent. "If you hadn't stopped me, something else would have."

Neither of them doubted that the moment was destined. Shane felt restraint fly away in the wind as she welcomed a spreading ache in her loins. Leaning against Dirk, she reveled in the pressure of his hands on her spine, expertly molding her to the pulsing planes of his body.

Possessed by the most intense craving of her life, she wound her arms around his thickly corded neck and sank with him into a pool of shade. Eager fingers opened her shirt and reached inside to cup the ripe fullness of her breasts. Shivers of anticipation flared out along her backbone as she felt the lift and swell of Dirk's manhood and the vibrant push of his body against hers.

"Shane, darling—"

His heated skin filled her nostrils with erotic perfume. His tongue teased the smooth, brown flesh of her shoulder as he peeled her shirt away.

With honeyed pleasure pouring through her, she lay back, lips parted, exulting in the excitement his nearness aroused, in the springy mass of his dark hair that was abrasive against the taut peaks of her breasts.

Blood pounding, she rode with him the keen edge of desire, savoring the cry of each heightened sense, letting the sexual tension build between them until she was panting in Dirk's grasp and the rasp of his breath was hot against her skin.

He knelt above her, bare and golden. "I want you, Shane."

She gave her assent, tumbling eagerly into the heart of his yearning. Their bodies merged. A moment of pure, blinding light—a heart-stopping moment—lifted them up and out of themselves. Weightless, timeless, their every nerve spoke. Shane shuddered, ecstatic, while Dirk clasped her to him, the plunging certainty of his thrusts claiming every inch of her.

Finally, linked breath by breath, they traveled the slow, downward spiraling of their passion until the descent enabled them to settle on a sea that held neither ripple nor wave, a placid glassy sea of deep fulfillment that kept them afloat while they drifted, deliciously sated and still, their bones water, their blood singing.

Dirk's lips moved along her throat, praising her. "My precious one . . . my Shane."

Her gaze melted over him. She thought in wonderment of her reluctance to arrive at this moment—this precious, beautiful, shining moment that made Dirk hers. No matter what happened now, they had shared a time so special, so natural and right that nothing could ever mar it. "Dirk," she whispered back.

The exchange of their names was to Shane like an exchange of vows. In Dirk's eyes she believed she read the same commitment she felt. He took her hands and held them to his lips, kissing her palms, her fingertips one by one, and then the smooth, sweet insides of her wrists where steady pulses beat out the state of her contentment.

When he took his lips away, Shane sighed and turned over on her stomach, soft laughter bubbling up from her chest. "We're a mess, did you know that? A gritty mess from head to foot."

"What a place to make love. You should have let me take you to a proper bed last night."

She turned over again, nibbling at his earlobe, reveling in her new freedom to do whatever she wanted. "Last night I was too proper to let you do that."

His steaming gaze moved over her slender length. "And now what are you?"

She stretched lazily, enjoying his heated appraisal. "I'm covered with sand fleas."

Startled, he peered at her more closely. "Good lord, you are!"

"So are you." Her cheeks dimpled as he swooped her up in his arms and started in long strides toward the water. "We're a traveling flea circus," she told the wind with a tinkle of laughter.

"But not for long." Dirk waded in until the rising surf reached his waist. Then, loosening his grasp, he let her slide down along his body into the nudging waves.

"Bye, bye, fleas," Shane said with a laugh, but her heart was hammering as fresh arousal swept over her.

Clinging together, they sank up to their shoulders, kissing, legs and arms entwined slickly beneath the surface, the spume salting their lips.

Shane closed her eyes to the golden sun and throbbed with love. *Love.* And this morning, only a few hours ago, she had been in despair—as Dirk had reminded her, on the verge of leaving. She recalled the scene at the breakfast table and laughed softly against Dirk's wet cheek. "Have you realized that you've put your head in the lion's mouth again?"

"The thought did occur to me. And I'm waiting," he answered thickly, binding her to him with knees tightly squeezing her narrow hips. "Devour me."

She made a growling sound and dropped a wet, lingering kiss on his lips, teasing the outline of his mouth with the tip of her tongue and a slow, tantalizing turning of her head.

A rasping moan broke from his throat. "Shane, you vixen." He dug his hands deep into the small of her back. Feeling him throb against her, she gave a delighted gasp and opened once more to him, welcoming the rush of his entry, closing in ecstasy around his thrusts.

Dirk. He filled her so completely . . . body, mind, and soul. She twisted ecstatically in his arms. Dirk belonged to her forever ... forever and forever.

Gradually the water stilled around them. They turned over and floated on their backs, fingers linked, glazed eyes feasting on the undulations of each other's nakedness beneath the water's shimmer.

"Happy?" Dirk murmured.

"Happy," she answered contentedly.

"It could have happened a long time ago, you know."

Shane was quiet, remembering the sensation she had experienced on the porch swing, the feeling that no matter how much he desired her, a part of him would stand away from their lovemaking. But today there had been no hint of reserve. It seemed incredible now that she could ever have imagined anything less than the joyous fulfillment he had given her.

She turned her gaze back to him, adoration spilling from her eyes. "I held back because it frightened me to think that another person had so much influence over me. But I'm not frightened anymore. You haven't made a prisoner of me, you've set me free." Her voice softened. "It's a miracle."

The day had been filled with miracles. In the space of only a few hours all her dreams had come true. On the shore a Spanish settlement that might make history lay waiting to be uncovered. But more important than that, she and Dirk had discovered each other. They had a history of their own to make—a history that she hoped would take a lifetime to unfold. Eager again for Dirk's kiss, she moved toward him through the water and brought her hungry lips to his.

Chapter Six

The week following the discovery of the Spanish settlement that had once thrived on Wanatoka was the most glorious Shane had ever experienced. Dirk seemed to live only to please her. It was hard to remember the surly stranger who had climbed up behind her saddle the day the blue-and-white Cessna dropped out of the dawn sky and frightened her mare.

The Dirk she knew now was never surly. He was witty and gentle, passionate and fun-loving. His eyes danced with tender mischief, or they melted her with hot desire. He was the friend who lightened every tedious task at the dig, the companion who could always make her laugh, the worker at her side who never tired. And in the soft, sweet hours they spent behind the closed door of her bedroom, he was her lover . . . the lover whose powerful body sliding toward her over the linen sheets transported her to realms of ecstasy she had only dreamed existed.

He was her first lover. She wasn't sure he was aware of that. She wasn't sure it mattered—to him, at least. A time to discuss it had never presented itself. There were too many other whisperings to share when he gathered her against his warm, furred chest. There was the strong, steady beat of his heart and the thrill of his hands stroking her flesh, teasing to tight peaks the rosy softness of her nipples, polishing her satin skin to a glow of arousal. There were his lips, shaping words of endearment against her eager mouth.

In the enfolding circle of his arms she knew a joy so great that she felt as radiant as the sun yielding to the moon. When they made love, the darkness around them exploded with stars, and deep inside her a symphony swelled, reached a crescendo, and then flowed like liquid gold throughout her body, making her feel beautiful and treasured and happier than she had ever imagined she could be.

Only one nagging fact marred her bliss. She knew that the euphoria she was experiencing was in all likelihood only a temporary state. Each day she dutifully reminded herself that in a few weeks she was scheduled to return to Texas. Then this brief, charmed time would be over.

At the dig on the first day they made love it had been easy to imagine that somehow she and Dirk might carve out a future together. In the most secret recesses of her heart she still cherished that hope. Her nights were filled with dreams of it. But the practical, daylight side of her nature wouldn't let her forget that the chance of that hope ever being realized was slim indeed.

The plans for her future were made, and nothing Dirk had said or done indicated that he was interested in altering them. As for his own plans, she wasn't privy to them. She only knew, with the instincts of one who senses the approach of devastating pain, that beyond Wanatoka the world Dirk moved in was not her world . . . and that these few precious days, slipping by like golden grains through an hourglass, would in all probability have to last her for a lifetime.

These ominous hauntings came sharply into focus one day at the start of the new week when a bank of dark, churning clouds rose in the east. Rain poured out of the sky. For a while Dirk roamed restlessly around the house, mourning the loss of a day at the dig. Then, soon after lunch, he disappeared.

Shane went to the library, telling herself how fortunate she was to have free time at last to transcribe some of her field notes onto her thesis cards. But the hours stretched out and she accomplished almost nothing. Every sound set her straining for Dirk's returning footsteps.

Soon she gave up altogether and fell into a dismal reverie that was the culmination of all she had kept at bay for a week. Dirk had become the focal point of her life. When they were together time flew. Apart from each other, it crawled. He had been away for only a few hours and already she was famished for the sight of his face, for the sound of his voice. How would she manage in a few weeks when she returned to the university and there was no possibility of ever seeing him again?

She had no answers for her questions, only the aching void inside her that reminded her of how vital it was to enjoy each moment she had left on the island, how necessary to her survival not to look ahead, but to hold on with all her might to the here and now because her life depended on it.

Finally, late in the afternoon, when the living-room windows were already darkening, she heard Dirk entering the foyer. In a moment his rangy body filled the doorway.

Leaping up, she rushed to him, not caring if it was obvious how much she needed him, not caring about anything except that he was home again, gathering her in his arms, holding her close.

"Umm—" He rubbed his nose along her cheek. "You smell wonderful."

"And you smell like a bog," she teased in relief. "Where have you been?"

"Nowhere in particular. Just roaming around, looking at things."

"Well, you'd better roam upstairs if you want a bath before Juno sounds the dinner gong."

"I think we'll go out for dinner." He drew back to gaze with approval at the mulberry-colored shift that clung appealingly to the supple lines of her body. "I know of a great restaurant in Savannah."

Shane laughed. "How will we get there? Swim? It's high tide. A plane can't land."

"A helicopter can. On the lawn." He headed out toward the stairs. "Don't go away. I'll be down again in twenty minutes."

"Dirk, wait—" She followed him into the hallway, frowning. "We aren't really going to Savannah, are we?"

"Of course."

"But Juno—I'm sure she has dinner ready here—"

"Juno isn't your worry. You've been cooped up long enough on this island. You need bright lights and music, or you'll be getting cabin fever, and then what will I do with you?"

"Kiss me?" she offered, but he only laughed and climbed another couple of stairs.

"No arguments, please. I'm the doctor, and I like happy patients."

His concern pleased her, but watching him disappear at the top of the stairs, she wished she had told him that nothing would make her happier than another of their long, pleasant evenings over books and wine right here in the library. The lights and music of Savannah were not nearly so appealing. It was more important than ever now to hoard every quiet hour she could spend with him, memorizing the shape of his head, the shape of his hands. When the time came for her to leave, she would need to carry with her memories of the way he sat when he pored over a book, memories of his voice reading her a passage, of his face and of his feet, of the way he moved toward the fire, of the hooded looks he sometimes gave her that were always a prelude to lovemaking.

She wanted to weep for the lost evening, but she knew Dirk's mind was made up. She was to be entertained whether she liked it or not.

The flight to Savannah was far from what Shane would have chosen, but despite her reluctance when they set out, the romance of being caught up in a swish and a roar from the lawn captivated her. She loved being at Dirk's side with the velvet night all around them. As they puttered along through the sky, the Georgia coast came into view. It stretched out for miles below them, twinkling with lights like a million dewdrops, the sparkling necklace that held back the Atlantic.

In almost no time at all the helicopter landed on the roof of a downtown hotel and then they were whisked in a glass elevator down to the dining room where an orchestra was playing. Champagne in a silver bucket appeared like magic at their table. Dirk ordered filet of trout sautéed in lemon and white wine, topped with shrimp and pine nuts. The dessert was an Old World gâteau with raspberry sauce and lemon custard peeking out from between the layers.

Dancing with Dirk provided a new excitement

Shane hadn't experienced on the island, and it was one, she thought, that she should have avoided at all costs if she ever meant to part with him. But once in his arms, she forgot about costs and let the pure joy of moving with him to the slow beat of the music count for everything.

Back at their table, he poured her another glass of champagne, and then suddenly all his ebullience left him. He stared at her face, softened by the candlelight, and said moodily, as if he were picking up in the middle of a conversation, "So, you see, Wanatoka needn't be considered an isolated, jumping-off place. Anytime one wants to escape, one can."

Shane stared back at him. "That's a new tack for you, isn't it?" she joked uncertainly. "Putting down Wanatoka?"

"I'm not." But his look stayed solemn. "If it were up to me, I'd never leave the island. I realize, however, that not everyone shares my views."

I share them, she told him silently. But he hadn't asked how she felt. One of her hardest tasks was to hide from him the depth of her feeling—for him and for his island, too. Every time he touched her, she yearned to pour out her desire to stay with him always. The long, lonely hours of the afternoon had pointed up graphically how entwined her life was with his, no matter how common sense argued against it. With every passing day her need for him grew.

But she bit back the words that burned at her lips, and replied like a dutiful guest, "This is a lovely place you've brought me to tonight. Thanks very much for a wonderful evening."

"One day soon we'll fly over to St. Simon's," he said, naming an island farther along the coast. "You mustn't go back to Texas without having at least one day at the Cloisters. There's Fort Frederika to visit, too, and John Wesley's church. Some of the finest examples of tabby houses are on St. Simon's."

"There are tabby houses on Wanatoka," she reminded him, thinking of the oyster-shell and lime-water dwellings she hadn't yet had a chance to explore.

But Dirk, roused now from his melancholy, had other proposals. "We might hop over to Jekyl for a day, too—"

"Dirk—" She couldn't restrain herself any longer. "You don't have to do this for me."

"Nonsense." He frowned. "I want to. I don't want you to be bored."

"I'm never bored on Wanatoka." Her eyes shimmered suddenly with tears of frustration. "There's so much on the island that I haven't absorbed yet. Kimbo's wife, Faymora, has invited me to tea. I want to meet Saphirra's family, too. And I never get enough of walking through the woods. Just being on the island is enough for me."

Dirk stared at her across the table. "Is it really?"

The look he gave her was so penetrating that she shrank from it. How prosaic he must think her. How dull, to turn down his glamorous plans in preference for a walk in the woods and tea with the wife of one of the servants.

Shane leaned forward anxiously. "Do you know what I'd like most of all when we have some free time?"

Her earnestness brought a smile to his lips. "Tell me. It's yours."

She was tempted in that instant to throw caution to the winds, to pour out her heart regardless of the consequences. But glancing around the crowded room and then back into Dirk's waiting face, she flushed, wondering if she would always be a fool, and she went on with what she had started to say.

"What I'd love is to do some of the things you enjoyed as a boy." She needed those memories, too, if she were to have the whole man to comfort her when she was half a world away from him. "Do you think we could, Dirk?"

Watching her, he relaxed. "What did you have in mind? Something like rattlesnake hunting?"

She bristled in the way that always made him smile. "I'm sure your father never let you do anything so dangerous."

"Shelling, then. How about that?"

"Yes! I'd love it." She clasped her hands excitedly, tasting the wind and the water already. "Are those your shells in the solarium? I've never thought to ask."

He nodded, captivated by the way she had begun to sparkle. "If it's calm tomorrow, we'll work at the dig in the morning and then take the rowboat over to the reef. That little blow we had this morning might have turned up some choice specimens."

"Dance with me one more time." She pushed back from the table, glowing with anticipation. "And then let's go home."

Chapter Seven

The shelling was spectacular on the reef the next day. In the first hour Shane had layered the bottom of her basket with exotic specimens. The air was still, as it had been the morning before, but the sky was cloudless. Rowing over in the boat, a distance Shane thought they might even have swum, Dirk had told her what she might expect to find, but even he was surprised at some of their discoveries.

They tramped happily along the sand, the water ruffling across their bare toes, until well after noon. Then in the shade of a half-tent Dirk had erected with sticks of driftwood and the tablecloth Juno had tucked into their lunch basket, they spread out a feast of hush puppies and corn on the cob that had cooked in a sand pit while they were shelling.

There were boiled peanuts, too, and mangoes, and a rare cluster of black grapes that inspired them to have a contest to see which of them could eat the most, the fastest, without swallowing any seeds.

After the last crumb of everything had disappeared, they stretched out in the shade to nap.

Between snoozes, Shane questioned drowsily, "Did you and Indigo ever come here?"

Dirk yawned. "Sometimes."

"All by yourself through all that water?"

"She was older, remember."

Shane raised up on one elbow for a better look at him. "How much older?"

"Four years—and wiser by another two."

Shane lay down again. "She can't have been very wise if she left Wanatoka."

A silence followed that started a queasy feeling in the pit of Shane's stomach. Once more she raised up to look at him. "Does that offend you? For me to criticize your sister?"

Dirk opened his eyes and gave her the full benefit of their unfathomable depths. "I can't think of anything you could do that would offend me."

Shane flushed, but to her disappointment Dirk failed to pursue the overture. Instead he went on about his sister.

"Indigo didn't leave the island of her own accord."

The tightness in his voice struck a warning in her ear. "Oh? What do you mean?"

"She left with my mother."

"I see."

"I doubt if you do." Then in a less caustic tone he added, "My father was a member of the cotton exchange. The house was often filled with buyers from the East." Another long pause followed and then he said quietly, "My mother went off with one of them. She took my sister with her."

"Oh, Dirk—" Stricken, Shane put out her hand. "I'm sorry."

"It doesn't matter. It was a long time ago." Dirk flipped a shell into the sea. "She never came back," he added tonelessly. "And neither did Indigo. Not even for Dad's funeral."

Shane's throat tightened as she thought of how he must have felt, losing his mother and his sister in one awful moment . . . a child with a sudden, unfillable void in his life. . . .

"But you kept in touch, didn't you?"

"Indigo wrote once or twice." He sat up, looping his arms loosely over his knees. "But Mother turned her against Wanatoka. Indigo regarded it as a prison. To me, it was a paradise. We didn't have much in common to sustain a correspondence."

Shane searched for words to express her sympathy. She was close to her own family, to one sister in particular. She couldn't imagine being cut off from any of them for the rest of her life. "Aren't you in contact now at all?"

"I've thought of ringing her up a couple of times when I've been in Switzerland on business. We had a mutual friend who gave me her number. But what would we have to say to each other? In Indigo's mind Wanatoka is a jungle. She could never understand how I feel about it."

Shane glanced around at the peacefully rocking boat, the golden sand, the basket of shells they had gathered. Wanatoka was as near heaven as a place could be. Her chin jutted out stubbornly. "I'm afraid I would never understand Indigo."

Dirk shrugged. "I don't imagine she's too different from most women."

"What do you mean?"

"Women thrive on excitement and glamorous surroundings. They require a setting where they can be admired."

The statement was so broad, so absurd, Shane laughed.

"Why is that amusing?"

"Because it's so insane! What's your basis for assumptions like that?"

"My mother's behavior," he answered stonily. "And Indigo's. The behavior, in fact, of women I've met in all parts of the world. I haven't known a one who could happily adapt to island life."

"I love the island," Shane said staunchly.

"Because you know you won't always have to stay here." He rose abruptly. "It's getting late. We'll go back now."

Shane felt shattered—by his tone and for other reasons as well. Earlier she had thought how beautiful the reef would be at sunset. She had envisioned Dirk making love to her in that peach-colored shimmer before night came on, she had imagined they might open their hearts to each other.

But Dirk's closed face told her that was out of

the question now. Their talk had touched a
nerve, and their beautiful day was over. Silently
she gathered up the picnic things. His last
remark had underlined what she already knew:
that he was entertaining no thoughts of their
being together beyond the time of her grant. She
understood now why he had hustled her off to
Savannah the evening before and why he was
making plans to take her other places. The
women in his experience were faithless, shallow
creatures whose only aim was self-gratification.
But what hurt worst of all was that he had classi-
fied her as one of them.

She rose, brushing the sand from her smoothly
tanned legs. "I'll wait in the boat while you take
down the tent."

Shane spent the next morning shut up in the
library though the sun was shining brightly and
Dirk came twice to the door to ask when she
would be ready to go to the dig.

At midmorning, when he appeared for the
third time, she said with an edge to her voice,
"Go on without me, why don't you?"

"Go without you?" He came into the room,
frowning. "What's wrong? Aren't you feeling
well?"

"Yes—I'm fine." But she did have a splitting
headache from lying awake half the night. At
dinner after they had come in from the reef she
had hardly been able to look at Dirk. An overwhelming sense of separateness made her feel

stiff and reserved. Fragments of the afternoon's conversation kept coming back, each time with more ominous overtones.

Somehow she had managed to get through the meal, and over coffee in the living room afterward, Dirk had been too preoccupied with his own somber thoughts to notice that she had nothing to say. But out on the lawn just before bed he finally observed how taciturn she had become.

"You're awfully quiet. Too much sun?"

"Too many stars," she answered, fighting an unsettling sense of *déjà vu*. The moment was so like the one they had experienced when they had walked Frances Forester home through the moonlight. Except that then Shane was only beginning to fall in love with Dirk, and now she could see nothing ahead for them beyond the spangle and dazzle of a temporary love affair that suddenly made her feel cheated and cheap, all in the same instant.

"Just look up there," she said morosely. "Millions and millions of lights."

"And millions more too far away for us to see them," Dirk agreed. "Do you know very much about the stars?"

"I don't know anything about them—except that they're beautiful and that I envy them."

Dirk seemed surprised. "Why?"

"Because they're fixed so permanently in their positions. They're not like people, drifting from one place to another."

"They change positions with the seasons, so they aren't as fixed as you think. And they have their own life expectancies, just as people do."

Shane turned to stare at his profile etched out against the blackness. "Do you mean stars die?"

He nodded. "Of course. Moment by moment through the aeons until finally their fires go out."

"And then what happens to them?"

"They turn into black cinders."

"All that lovely light?" She shivered, chilled by the similarity between the ice-blue glitterings above them and their own relationship, burning out now into its own little heap of cinders and ashes. "I think that's dreadful."

"Do you?" He stared at her. "You're an idealist if you look for constancy in anything."

Shane sucked in her breath. "And you're a gray-bearded pessimist if you don't."

On that note they had parted—Dirk stalking silently back to the library to read, and Shane going to lie for hours in bed, staring at the ceiling while sleep eluded her.

But now as Dirk came toward the library table where she sat, he seemed to have forgotten her angry words.

"Are you sure you're all right?" He pulled her up from her chair. Curving his hands around her shoulders, he drew her against him with an air of possessiveness that wiped out for a moment the dark thoughts that had haunted her lonely hours. In his eyes she saw a protective tenderness mingling with a glow of naked desire that she found hard to cope with on this upsetting morning.

"Please don't look at me like that."

He smiled. "How am I looking at you?"

She managed a shaky laugh. "As if you might eat me."

"I want to." His voice thickened. "Every time I touch you, I want to." One hand tightened at her nape. The other pressed suggestively into her spine. "I never get enough of you."

After the torturous things she had been thinking, his words fell like music on her ears. But deliberately she took herself out of his arms. There were servants all over the house. Saphirra was cleaning her room upstairs. In the hall, a whistling Timotheus polished a brass fern stand. There was nowhere they could go to finish what Dirk seemed intent on starting.

Playfully she reminded him, "Have you forgotten this is a workday?"

He slid his hands down and encircled her waist. "I forget everything when I'm with you."

Shane felt her resistance melting. He was so easy to love, so stimulating, so desirable. A kind fate somewhere must have saved him just for her. But if that were true, why didn't Dirk know it too? In a few weeks would he let her go and *never* know?

"Dirk—" She remembered suddenly what she had been thinking of for days and had kept pushing to the back of her mind. It had to be discussed, and this would be as good a time as any.

"Actually, I think it would be best if neither of us went to the dig today."

"Why?" He nuzzled her neck. "Would you rather go to St. Simon's?"

"I don't want to go anywhere." She took his arms down from her shoulders. "I want to talk. I have something to say."

"Sounds serious," he mocked. But he settled his weight on the corner of the table and folded his arms expectantly. "Well, go on. What is it?"

The speech she had made up for this occasion came obligingly to her lips. "An archaeological site, especially one based in sand, presents an extremely fragile situation."

He gave an exaggerated yawn. "Is that so? Couldn't we talk about the weather?"

"Please, Dirk, this is important."

He grinned sheepishly. "Sorry. But when you get pedantic, you're a terrible bore, did you know that?"

"You're making this very difficult."

"Okay, okay, don't get upset. You have my undivided attention. Please go on."

She cleared her throat self-consciously. "On a dig such as the one we've been working on, one wrong footstep could wipe out something irreplaceable. We've been very lucky so far, but—" She took a long breath, instinctively anticipating his displeasure. "But I think the time has come when we have to turn the dig over to a team of experts."

"Experts?" His smile faded. "Someone from the outside, do you mean?"

"Of course someone from the outside." She gave a teasing lilt to her words to soften their impact, but she knew exactly how he was feeling. She felt the same way herself, and for that reason she had put off broaching the subject longer than she should have. The dig was their private domain. It was where they had made love for the first time . . . where they spent every day, alone, and in absolute bliss. She knew how wrenching it was to suggest opening that domain to intruders. But it had to be done. The professional side of her feared that they had already gone on too long playing like children in the sand. The discovery they had made was too significant for them to endanger it in any way.

Reluctantly she began again. "I'm acquainted with the work of Professor Mitterand at the Museum of Natural History in New York. I've been thinking that if we contacted him—"

In a surprising burst of anger Dirk cut her off. "We don't need Professor Mitterand—or anyone else." He verified his assertion by motioning toward the far end of the room where a tabletop was covered with the artifacts they had unearthed. "We're doing fine on our own."

"We've only scratched the surface, Dirk."

"Then later, if we need to, we can call in someone."

He was taking her suggestion much harder

than she had imagined, and a little flag of hope unfurled inside her. Perhaps their relationship was more important to him than he had realized. Gently she pleaded with her eyes. "I'm afraid later is already here. You know, in less than two weeks my grant expires."

"We'll work something out," he resisted stubbornly. "We'll get an extension. You can finish your thesis here."

Shane's lips parted. "What? What do you mean?" Over the hammering of her heart, her thoughts raced. He was asking her to stay on—

But in his next breath, Dirk made himself clear. "I'll be here until the first of June. You can stay too. When we're ready to leave, we'll discuss bringing in someone else to see to the dig."

Shane clenched her hands at her sides in an attempt to steady herself. He wanted her to stay on, but only until his vacation was over. He only wanted a convenient, acquiescent lover he could discard when he was ready to move out into the world again.

"I can't finish my thesis here. I could never get university approval for that." She swallowed past the tightness in her throat, determined not to let him see how badly he had wounded her.

"But regardless of any other consideration," she told him evenly, "the mission site is far too valuable and important to risk any longer in the hands of amateurs."

She wasn't prepared for the angry flush that

rushed to his cheeks. "If I've been clumsy at the dig, you should have said so before now."

"You haven't been clumsy. If anything, you're more careful than I am. What I'm trying to say— and saying it badly, I suppose—is that the site is out of our league now." With dogged determination she kept her thoughts off her personal anguish. "For the work that lies ahead, I'm just as much an amateur as you are."

His chin jutted. "Amateurs or not, you and I are the only ones who are going near that site. We can either close it down altogether or go on exactly as we have been. When it's time for us to leave, we'll discuss the pros and cons of calling in experts. But until then, I won't have anyone coming on the island."

Shane stared up at him with a look of astonishment, every thought but one flying from her head. "That sounds like a command."

"Interpret it any way you want, as long as you understand my meaning."

"I could hardly do otherwise, could I?" She took a step back, feeling sick and disoriented. Who was this granite-faced man issuing orders? From her dry throat she brought up a challenge. "I wonder if you realize how unreasonable you're being."

"I can afford to be unreasonable. I own Wanatoka."

"You don't own history! No one does. And no one has the right to impede discoveries that are a part of it."

Resentment flared in his eyes. "I can do anything I like on my own land."

"I thought Wanatoka was a corporation. What about Juno and Kimbo? Timotheus and Saphirra, and all the others? They're stockholders, aren't they? Doesn't it matter what they think?"

"You didn't worry about what they were thinking when you let me into your bedroom, did you?"

Shane gasped.

Instantly the pain of regret darkened his eyes. He stepped forward and gripped her shoulders. "That was a rotten thing to say, Shane. I'm sorry." He made a move to draw her closer, but she twisted free, trembling violently, and ran toward the door.

"Shane, wait—"

She heard him coming after her and darted quickly around a corner and into a darkened recess in the hall. When he thundered past, she emerged and ran blindly in the opposite direction.

Chapter Eight

Drifts of wild hyacinths were blooming in the sunlit clearings of the forest. Sweet bay trees gave off their spicy aroma, lilies nodded in damp bogs, and Carolina jasmine perfumed the air, but Shane was conscious of nothing but the unfamiliar path skimming by under her feet as she rushed through the undergrowth that led away from the mansion.

How had she ever imagined she loved Dirk? How could the caresses of so heartless a man ever have aroused her?

Her skin burned as she thought of herself opening to him like the white flower she snatched from the edge of the path and snapped from its fragile stem. She had bared herself to him in every private way, believing he had done the same, wanting to believe, making herself believe. Not that he hadn't warned her. His cool withdrawal on the reef, that had been a warning. His moments of reserve before that—

Sickened, she thought of how her infatuation

97

with him had blinded her to what he was really like—a selfish savage!

She halted in the path, tears streaming down her face. This beautiful island world she longed to call her home forever belonged to a brute whom she had actually hoped to marry! She had come so close to throwing over all her plans, to abandoning all her goals just to be with him.

Sinking down on a rock, she brushed at her tears angrily. Then she heard him coming, thrashing through the undergrowth, until suddenly he burst out into the clearing in front of her.

"Shane!" He came toward her swiftly. "Lord, how did you ever find this remote place?" Pulling her up, he wrapped her in a fierce embrace that took her breath away. "I've made you cry," he murmured thickly. "Do you hate me?"

"Yes, I hate you!" A fresh rush of tears flooded her cheeks. "I don't want to ever see you again."

Bending, he kissed the wet paths that streaked her face. He kissed her cold lips and the insides of her wrists. "I've hurt you terribly, but it's all right now, sweetheart. It was a bad dream, a nightmare. I went mad for a minute and now I'm sane again."

"Do you think that makes up for anything? I'll never forgive you."

"You shouldn't." The reassuring sounds from his lips fell like rain on her raw senses. "I said a rotten thing to you. I behaved like a tyrant back there in the library. Whatever you're thinking, I deserve it."

"Yes, you do."

"But be generous, can't you, darling?" The magic was back in his voice, its dulcet tones hypnotizing her. "Make allowances for impulsiveness, for my wanting to keep you all to myself for as long as I could, no matter what lengths I had to go to."

The scent of his skin, his heated body so close to her, worked insidiously to tear down her resistance. "Please," she moaned, "don't touch me."

He breathed hotly against her throat. "I have to touch you. You're irresistible. You have been since the moment I laid eyes on you in that pink silk dress with your puritan look daring me to come close to you." Cradling her in his arms, he kissed her damp forehead. "You look so lovely when you cry."

Suddenly the air went out of her, and she dropped her head on his chest and gasped out in a muffled blur of words, "You made me feel so horribly cheap, Dirk."

"I know." His lips moved in her hair. "I meant to."

She recoiled as if he had slapped her, but he held her fast and spoke quickly in the low, hoarse way she could never resist. "Without even wincing, you put a finish to the most precious hours I've ever spent. It hurt. I wanted to hurt you back, like a child."

"But you're not a child. What right have you to behave like one?"

"How does a man behave when he's enchanted?" His searching gaze burned into her. "You can't hate me for doing anything I could to keep you to myself."

"What I hate is your domineering air." Her voice cracked. "I hate—"

"Hate anything but me." He put his lips to hers. She tried to hold back the response he aroused, but as always, the power in the movement of his mouth wouldn't be denied.

When at last she drew back from him, limp and throbbing, she confessed brokenly, "I feel so—so torn."

"Don't—not any longer. I tell you it's all right." His lips moved against hers as he talked. "We'll do what you want. We'll go back to the house and I'll signal the mainland for a plane. In Savannah you can call your professor."

Shane pulled back. "You'd let me do that? After what you said? How could you have changed your mind so quickly?"

"I haven't really." Her gaze jumped to meet his. "I'll do what you want," he told her, "because _you_ want it, not because I do. I despise the idea of hordes of strangers invading Wanatoka."

All at once her heart overflowed with love for him. "Oh, Dirk—it won't be like that."

"It will."

"No—the team from the museum will be highly trained professionals." She laid her hands on his shoulders, longing to chase the desolate look from his eyes. "They won't mar anything on the island."

"Their presence alone will mar it."

"Scholars have been coming to Wanatoka for years," she pleaded. "What about them?"

"They've never been a menace because they're controlled by a well-thought-out set of rules."

"You can make rules for the archaeological team too."

"And what about the press?"

Shane blinked. She hadn't thought about the demands of the media. But he was right, of course. The mission site was a major discovery. Once the word was out, there would be no way to keep it from the press. "We'll work out something." Shane licked her lips. "The remoteness of the island will help."

Dirk's soft, scoffing laughter cut into her. "There's not a corner on earth that a television camera can't squeeze itself into."

"That may be true," she admitted reluctantly, "but I'm sure we can keep the invasion to a minimum. Professor Mitterand, or whoever he sends out, will help us. Oh, Dirk—" She was weak suddenly with relief that none of the awful things she had been thinking about him were true. "I'm so glad you understand."

His gaze traveled slowly over her, and again she saw the desolate look that haunted her. "I've always understood. Since the day you plucked the first medallion out of the sand."

Her eyes filled with unexpected tears. "So I'm to blame. All your misery is my fault."

He reached out and pulled her to him. "My misery and my joy." In a roughened voice he added, "If I can't have one without the other, I'll take them both and be glad of it."

"Oh, Dirk." She lifted her lips to his. "It will all be fine. You'll see. Trust me."

Ch

Shane was unprepared for
Savannah Dirk showed her, its quiet, shady
streets broken, block after block, by quaint green
squares. Neither had she anticipated her
response to its restored mansions, its splashing
fountains, and its heroic statues centering the little parks. She couldn't stop exclaiming over its
loveliness.

"You didn't see it on your way to Wanatoka?"
Dirk asked as they walked in the early evening.

"I had hoped to, but there wasn't time. Oh,
look—the Owens-Thomas House." Eagerly she
matched the location on her map with the fine
example of Regency architecture they were
passing. "If it's open tomorrow, can we go
inside?"

"Of course." Dirk smiled at her childlike
enthusiasm and enclosed her hand more
securely in his. "We'll have plenty of time to see
everything."

Shane agreed. A whole day to themselves lay
ahead while they waited for Professor Mitterand

hane had called the museum
essor had been dubious about
on. Who was Shane McBride to
alized in panic. But when Dirk got on
Mitterand was making plans within
its.

he Dirksen Foundation talks," she had
ased in a stage whisper, but she could hardly
contain her excitement when Dirk told her after
he hung up that the professor and a colleague
would be flying in to return with them to
Wanatoka.

But best of all, she had regained her confidence in Dirk. In the flurry of leaving the island, she hadn't let herself think of the ugly scene in the library or even of their reconciliation in the forest. But by the time she was soaking in a hot tub in the suite Dirk had engaged for her at Creedmoor House, an excellent little inn near Christ Church, she was better able to put into perspective the upset of the morning.

Dirk was right: it was a bad dream, a childish reaction in a man who might be falling in love, even if he didn't know it yet.

Shane had smiled then and closed her eyes as the steam from her bath rose around her. She hadn't been fair breaking to him her thoughts about the dig "without even wincing," as he termed it. She should have been more tactful, more considerate of his feelings.

She smiled again now at Dirk as he walked beside her. It was flattering too, in retrospect, that his first reaction had been to want to keep her all to himself for a little while longer. How would she have felt if he had gone on up to the end offering no resistance to her impending departure?

Dirk slipped an arm around her waist. "What does that self-satisfied smile mean?"

The warm intimacy in his tone stirred up a glow within her, and she breathed happily of the soft, spring evening. She was glad she had worn the lilac silk blouse Dirk liked and the trim mauve skirt that molded her figure in a becoming way. She was glad simply to be alive. "I'm smiling because I'm happy that I'm here with you."

"No bad thoughts about this morning?"

"I've forgotten about it," she answered airily. "So should you."

He shook his head. "I made you unhappy. I never intend to do that again."

In an effort to lighten his mood she teased, "Think of our quarrel as an electrical storm. It cleared the air."

He gave her a wry smile. "I wasn't aware that the air needed clearing."

"There's so much we still don't know about each other, Dirk." She went on without noticing the closed look that came over his face. "We're bound to step on each other's toes now and then."

"I suppose you're right." But he changed the

subject at once. "I think it's time to concentrate on where we're going to have dinner."

Shane glanced toward a series of long, low buildings that lay ahead on the bluff at the river's edge. Factor's Row it was called on the guidebook map, a grouping of old cotton warehouses that now held fashionable boutiques, taverns, and restaurants—everything that a tourist might enjoy. "What about something down there?"

"Tomorrow perhaps." Dirk took her elbow and steered her firmly toward the corner. "Tonight I think Pirates' House is the place for us."

Shane thought so too the minute she caught sight of the building that Dirk told her was the oldest in the state.

"Two hundred years ago it was an inn," he said when they were seated inside; the decor was entrancing in its buccaneer flavor. "It was a rendezvous for pirates then. Did you notice the Jolly Roger on the flagpole outside?"

"Yes, I did. But I didn't know the place was genuine."

Dirk chuckled. "Almost everything in Savannah is genuine. The city is like a lovely Southern lady who's been asleep for a hundred years. Recently she's roused herself and discovered that she's grown old with grace and beauty."

Shane's expression softened. "I hope one day something as nice as that happens to me."

He reached across the table and covered her

small hand with his. "Everything nice should happen to you."

He might have said more, but a platter of seafood arrived. Crab claws and boiled shrimp, flounder fried crispy brown, and little fried oysters. It was a banquet for Shane, who loved the Georgian method of preparing food.

While they ate, their talk was lighthearted and pleasant and centered mostly around the interesting prospect of watching Professor Mitterand and his colleague take in the enormity of their discovery.

By the time they were out on the street again, strolling back toward Creedmoor House, the sense of well-being Shane had enjoyed before their outing on the reef had been completely restored.

At her door she handed Dirk her key, anticipating with a feverish rise of excitement the moment when he would take her in his arms again. But when they were in the little sitting room that adjoined her bedroom, Dirk said casually, "What would you think about contacting Mitterand in the morning before he leaves New York? There's no real rush about his coming, is there?"

Shane stared. "Dirk—it's all settled."

"I know." He smiled engagingly. "But we could unsettle it, couldn't we? The mission site has lain there for four hundred years. What will a few more weeks matter? The islanders already know not to go near it, and now that I understand your point of view, I'll stay away too. Then when it's time for us to leave—"

"We've been all through this."

His look darkened. "I can't seem to get across to you how much Wanatoka is going to change once this news gets out. If you understood, you'd want to put it off as much as I do."

"What *I* understand is that you're overreacting terribly." She crossed swiftly to his side. "You're obsessed with Wanatoka being destroyed. Can't you see that the purpose of calling in help is to preserve a part of the island? Of course things won't be quite the same for a while. There'll probably be some press coverage, a few strands of sea oats may get trampled, but everything important is going to remain intact."

"Is it?" Her angry tone seemed to raise his own ire. "Can you guarantee that?"

"I think I can—as nearly as anything in this world can be guaranteed. At least I'll promise you this: I'll certainly do my best to preserve Wanatoka exactly as it is." Her voice broke suddenly and she reached out for him. "Oh, Dirk, why can't you accept the fact that I love the island almost as much as you do? I know how important every blade of grass is to you. Don't you know me well enough by now to believe that I'd never do anything that would jeopardize its peace and serenity?"

He took her in his arms then. But when he had kissed her, he said, "Sleep well." And he went off down the hall toward his own room.

Shane did not sleep well, and the next morning at eight, when Dirk tapped on her door, she rushed to open it, her brow furrowed anxiously.

But when he saw her, he smiled as if there had been nothing unusual in their parting. His amused gaze traveled over her sleep-tossed hair as he bent to drop a light kiss on her lips. "I thought you wanted to get an early start on seeing the town."

A trifle miffed, Shane answered, "When the alarm went off, I was just shutting my eyes." She stepped aside to let him enter and then added with a bold thrust of her chin, "You were in such a hurry to get away after dinner that I stayed awake half the night wondering why."

"I'm sorry." Effortlessly he pulled her into his arms. "We'd had such a strenuous day, I thought you wanted to rest."

Shane melted against him, welcoming with a quiver of desire the passage of his hands between the thin folds of her dressing gown.

"I can never stay angry at you," she murmured helplessly.

"Good." His tone roughened. "Are you sure you want to go touring?"

Her mouth went slack against his. "Not as sure as I was before you knocked. But you're all dressed, ready to go."

His voice thickened. "I could get undressed."

"Then we'd get a late start." But her fingers

were already opening the buttons of his shirt, her lips nibbling at his with tantalizing eagerness.

Deftly he slipped her robe from her shoulders. Moving with her in his arms to the bedroom, he lay down beside her in the hollow of the bedcovers, still warm from her body. In a long, caressing motion he brought her nightgown up over her head.

Where she had opened his shirt, dark chest hair curled thickly. She nestled her cheek against it, shaken by the sheer maleness of him, still clothed against her nakedness.

Then, with a stab of delight she understood that he meant for her to undress him. A new kind of ecstasy seized her and she unclasped his belt buckle and slipped her hands onto the warm flesh beneath it.

His rasping groan told her that it was no longer a game for him. But it was Shane's turn to play games now. With deliberate slowness she took off each piece of his clothing, meticulously folding it in front of his fevered gaze before she set it aside. She was torturing herself too, but it was a torture that enhanced the raging need within her. Finally she bent her head and trailed a row of moist, trembling kisses along his inner thigh.

Dirk gasped and locked her to him. Shane arched against him, reveling in his embrace. Then, in a blaze of unleashed passion more exquisite than anything either had ever known before, their striving peaked.

When they were quiet at last, Shane lay back, listening to the pounding of her heart, picturing it as a caged bird that only Dirk could free. In a silent, silver stream, the elixir of his lovemaking coursed through her. He was hers . . . she was his . . . for all their days to come. There could be no question about it now. Nothing was as important as their being together. All that was left on this blissful plateau of fulfillment was for him to say so. . . .

Then gradually the world came back into focus. Shane saw the sun on the windowsill, her suitcase open on a chair. Gazing across the rumpled sheets at Dirk's dark eyes gazing back at her, she confessed, "Yesterday, when I ran away from you into the woods, I never thought you would hold me again."

He put out his hand and stroked damp wisps of hair back from her forehead. "I thought we were going to forget all that."

"Maybe we can't forget it until we talk about it." She trailed a finger down the bridge of his nose. "You weren't at all like yourself. Not like you are now."

He gave her a steamy look. "If this is how you like me best—" He reached for her again, but she shoved back from him, laughing.

"You're insatiable."

"And you, my sweet Shane," he taunted with narrowed eyes, "are a tease."

Her smile faded slowly. For a minute she played with his fingertips, kissing their strong, rounded tips. Then she said quietly, "I'm sorry that you have such a poor regard for women."

"For women in general," he said lightly, and nipped at the end of her nose with his even white teeth.

"Don't joke. I'm serious."

"So am I." He lay back and looked at the ceiling. "You won't like hearing me say so, I know, but most of the women I've met are undependable, unpredictable, and totally wrapped up in themselves. If they have a career, you can multiply that by two."

Shane sat up. "I'm a woman with a career."

"Present company excepted, of course." But when he came up on his elbow, he wasn't smiling. "However, you won't deny, will you, that you find your career very absorbing?"

"Some phases of it," she admitted, conscious of a clammy feeling spreading over her skin. "But it isn't my whole life."

"Have you ever really put that to a test?"

"I don't have to. I know." She brought her chin up. "I'm a woman first. Then I'm an archaeologist."

"That doesn't leave much room for anything else."

Her heart began a slow thumping. "What else have I left out?"

"You prove my point if you have to ask."

"If you mean marriage, children—I want all that."

He gave her a thoughtful look. "But only when

it's convenient, isn't that right? And if it doesn't interfere with anything else?"

She flushed. "That's your conclusion, not mine."

He lay down again. "Shall I tell you how I reached it?"

She looked at him turned on his side, the long line of his tanned torso facing her, making a sensuous contrast to the snowy sheets. A warning signal went off in her brain: It doesn't matter . . . don't spoil this lovely hour.

"Well?" His voice held a note of challenge. "Shall I tell you? Or shall we forget this disruptive conversation and get back to more important issues?"

She moistened her lips. "Maybe there isn't anything more important than this."

For an instant longer he delayed. Shane held her breath, studying his generous mouth, sculpted and still in his craggy face.

Then in a cool, expressionless voice he said, "The day I met you on the beach was my wedding day."

Shane's hand flew to her lips.

"The ceremony never came off, of course." His mouth twisted in a sardonic smile. "Instead, I spent the day flying over the ocean. I realized just in time that my bride-to-be was possessed of all those charming atrributes so common to her gender." His eyes moved over Shane's chalky cheeks. "It was clear all of a sudden that our only bond was a year of meeting in exotic places and attending extravagant, senseless parties." He lifted his shoulders in a jarring show of contempt. "So in Hong Kong, just before I returned to Wanatoka, I bowed out."

Shane stared at him, unable to reconcile the earth-shaking violence of this moment with the hour of ecstasy that had preceded it. "Who—?" Her voice rasped out. "Who was the bride?"

"One of those 'women in general.' Patrice Page, by name. You may have seen her photograph. Last month in all the magazines she was the Shangri-la perfume girl."

A vivid memory of slender legs, dark hair, and limpid, wide-set eyes sprang up in Shane's mind. "The girl on the tiger skin?" she said in a small, choked voice.

He nodded. "One of the world's highest-paid models. It's hard to believe now that I was ever involved with her. I haven't any feelings at all for Patrice." His gaze lost its focus. "I suppose I never did have."

"You planned to marry her."

He shrugged. "I was drifting. She held out an anchor."

Shane couldn't stop staring. All the time she was falling in love with him he was remembering the shape of another woman in his arms.

"Wherever I went," she heard him going on, "Patrice was there, dazzling everyone. All those seemingly coincidental meetings were planned. But at the time I wasn't aware of that."

He was aware of Patrice's lips, Shane thought starkly. Of her eyes. Of her satin-smooth body.

Suddenly Dirk leaned forward and placed a kiss on Shane's icy lips. "There's no reason for you to look so unhappy. What I'm telling you has nothing to do with us—except that you wanted to know how I formed my conclusions about women's deviousness and their careers."

Shane's voice shook. "If she was so interested in following you around the world, she couldn't have been too interested in her career."

"She thought that because I traveled a lot, I wouldn't object if she did the same—whenever and in whatever direction money called her. She didn't know about Wanatoka. When she found out that I planned for us to spend most of our free time there, she let me know I'd be spending it by myself. I began waking up then. In a few days I called it quits."

Shane turned away, pulling the bedcovers up to her chin.

His face stilled. "I never loved her, Shane."

In a voice racked with pain she said, "You asked a woman you didn't love to marry you? I don't understand that kind of behavior."

"I don't understand much about love." Sliding an arm under her shoulder, he turned her over against his bare chest. "I was looking for someone to fill an emptiness in my life." His luminous gaze reached out for her. "I didn't know when I was making plans with Patrice that not just anyone could fill that emptiness."

Shane's voice trembled. "You're a sophisticated man. I can't believe you're as naive as that."

"It's true nevertheless." His lips trailed along the line of her jaw, teasing at her resistance. He had such power over her, power in his voice, his mouth, his hands. Even the dark lashes that fringed his eyes played a part in her undoing. Everywhere their flesh touched, her nerves responded with anguished longing.

"Dirk—"

He covered her mouth in a deep, plundering kiss. She floundered for a moment, helpless under its spell, and then she pushed away from him.

"Whatever I shared with Patrice is over, Shane," he muttered hoarsely. "I shouldn't have told you."

"I think I have a right to know. Do you think you can drop a bomb like that and in the next minute expect me to make love with you?"

"You want to make love with me."

"I want to hear about the woman you almost married!"

He sat up abruptly, pulling her with him. "All right, then—listen. She's twenty-nine years old. She paints her toenails pink and she reads Agatha Christie mysteries in bed." He held Shane immobile in a hard embrace. "Yes, I've been to bed with her. Any more questions?"

A cry wrenched from Shane's throat. "I've never been to bed with anyone but you."

"Oh, God," he rasped hoarsely, "don't you

think I know that? Don't you know how precious, how sacred that trust is to me?" He took her face between his hands, kissing her lips feverishly. "You're my treasure, Shane."

She twisted away. "Don't. This isn't the time. I'm too mixed up, too confused."

His hold on her loosened. His dark eyes searched her face. "Because of Patrice?"

"Because of everything. It's all happened too fast." She moved out of his arms and drew her knees to her chest in a shuddering motion. "Wanatoka must have cast a spell on me."

Dirk's eyes glowed hotly. "Then let it work."

"It's been working too long already." She turned her dazed face on him. "I should have left at Easter when everyone else did." She had misunderstood everything. Dirk would never say, Stay with me for as long as you live. He had made her believe he loved her, but it was a woman he didn't love whom he had asked to marry him. "I belong in Texas," she choked out. "The sooner I go back there and finish my degree, the better."

She closed her eyes tightly for a moment, and when she opened them again, Dirk was out of bed, pulling on his clothes.

He turned around with a stony look when he felt her stare. "Do you want to go sight-seeing or not?"

Savannah . . . she had forgotten it even existed.

"Yes—yes I want to go." Numbly she searched through the tumbled bedclothes for her dressing gown, trying to block out the harshness in his tone. He was going to let her leave without even an argument. Until this moment she had never known how much she needed him . . . and he didn't need her at all. His treasure? What a joke!

She watched him saunter to the window. Women were all the same to him. His mother, his sister, the model he had walked out on in Hong Kong . . .

For a minute she pitied Patrice Page. She pitied all the women he had ever known. The story Dirk had told her was the story of his life. The women who passed through it were of no more significance than clouds.

Dirk turned around, his face set. "You said your career wasn't everything."

"It isn't." Her blurred gaze stayed on the gauzy fabric she was drawing around her nakedness. "But at the moment it's at the top of my list."

"I see." His hands clenched into fists at his sides. "Nothing must be allowed to impede the course of history. Isn't that how you put it yesterday?"

She had spoken those words in anger . . . anger was all he remembered out of all their beautiful days. A scorching pain seared her. In a voice as coldly remote as his she said, "At least history endures."

Reaching into her suitcase, she brought out a handful of filmy underthings. "Would you mind waiting in the other room until I'm dressed."

Chapter Ten

Professor James Mitterand was an authoritative, distinguished-looking white-haired man. But his colleague—a woman—was young, petite, dressed in a beautifully tailored black suit, and as articulate as she was attractive. She and Dirk had traveled to many of the same places in the world, and on the flight back to Wanatoka they shared a seat, chatting almost constantly while Shane did her best to concentrate on the low, cultured voice of the man beside her. But by the time they were nearing the island, her neck was stiff from straining to hear what Dirk and Lois were saying behind her and to listen at the same time to the professor.

The day before, while she and Dirk waited in Savannah for the arrival of the two archaeologists from New York, the hours had stretched out endlessly. Like a polite stranger, Dirk had led her about the town. But none of the interesting old houses she had looked forward to seeing held any charm for Shane. The words of the tour guides bounced dully off her ears, while in her breast a turmoil raged. The aloof smile she had determinedly pasted on her lips to match Dirk's had her face aching long before lunchtime.

But hardest to bear was Dirk's casual and assured manner as he steered her from one attraction to the next. He gave no sign that the day was not everything he expected it to be. At sunset, when he wanted to prolong it with a boat ride down the river, Shane finally rebelled.

"Go by yourself," she all but shouted. "I'm exhausted."

Her show of anger cracked the facade of civility that had seen them through the day. Dirk's suavity turned to concern as he hailed a taxi. "Why didn't you say something sooner?"

"You were having such a wonderful time," she retorted, "I didn't want to spoil it." Then she walked off, leaving him to get rid of the taxi and chase after her.

He caught up with her at the corner. "Stop behaving like a four-year-old." His voice hoarsened. "You might give a little thought to how the day began, Shane."

She tightened her lips. "I'd rather jump in front of a bus."

"You're being foolish, absurd."

"I'm being myself! Not everyone can be dazzling, you know."

He swore softly. "What are you jealous of? I told you exactly how I feel about Patrice."

"And I understand perfectly. Will you just leave me alone?"

"Gladly." His own mouth tightened. "But first we have to get through dinner."

"You're dreaming if you think I have any plans of eating it with you."

She swung around and marched off toward Creedmoor House, but his long strides brought him even with her before she had gone more than a few feet.

Whirling her around, he snapped out, "I've never seen you like this."

Tears clogged her throat. She had never felt like this. "That should make you doubly glad you're rid of me for the evening."

His jaw hardened. "I don't want to be rid of you."

But when they reached the inn, he went straight to the desk and she heard him ordering dinner for one, sent up to the room she occupied.

Climbing the stairs, she told him hotly, "I suppose it never occurred to you that I might not care for poached salmon and parsleyed potatoes."

"I ordered the specialty of the house," he said stonily.

"That's very thoughtful, I'm sure, except that parsely makes me itch and I detest those mushy little bones in salmon filets."

"Then, if you like, pitch the whole business out the window." Without another glance he stalked off toward his own room at the other end of the hall.

Breakfast the next morning was no less a strain. They ate at separate tables in the small dining room, ignoring the curious glances of the waiters. Both Shane and Dirk were grateful that within the hour the professor and Lois Traylor were due to arrive.

"So this is Wanatoka." Smiling, Lois Traylor set her shiny patent-leather pumps on the hard-packed sand of the beach.

Shane wondered angrily why she hadn't worn a satin gown with a train as well. It would have been about as appropriate for the island as the black suit that molded her trim figure. But immediately she realized how childish she was being. The petitely attractive woman whose hand lay in the crook of Dirk's arm was no more to blame for the wretchedness she felt than was Professor Mitterand, offering his own arm to her as they crossed the sand.

But she was so depressed that even the moss-draped oaks towering over them as they entered the woods irritated her. She wanted to do something so shocking and terrible it would wipe the civilized smiles off all their faces. She wanted to beat her fists on Dirk's broad chest and make him admit what a rotten, shallow, self-centered individual he really was.

But in spite of the storm raging inside her, she walked along at the professor's side, calmly answering the questions he put to her concerning the dig and nodding agreeably when Dirk occasionally added a comment.

When they reached the house, she made herself do penance by acting the hospitable hostess in the solarium and then showing Lois to her room and summoning Saphirra for an introduction.

"All you need to do here is ask for what you want," she told Lois when Saphirra was gone. "It appears at once, like magic. And the food is wonderful too." She was sorry that her voice lacked warmth, but there seemed to be nothing she could do about it. Thankfully, Lois appeared not to notice.

The other woman had sat down on the edge of the snowy bedspread. Now she commented brightly, "Every archaeologist dreams of a find like you've made. How does it feel?"

"All kinds of ways." Shane hid her turmoil by looking out toward the ocean. "It was like the Fourth of July at first, with skyrockets exploding. That first medallion—I couldn't believe what I held in my hand. It was overwhelming"—her voice trailed off—"humbling."

And then, dear Lois, she thought with an ache, Dirk and I made love and nothing else mattered.

She took a long breath to shake off the memory. "Most of all, I realize how inadequate I am to deal with it."

Lois couldn't know she was speaking of more than the dig. "I doubt that anyone who comes to work on the Wanatoka site will feel much different than you do. On every dig we learn. And on one such as this promises to be, the opportunities are endless for finding out just how little we know of the vastness of things."

Shane swallowed against the tightness in her throat. Lois was really quite nice, she admitted guiltily. And the professor too. He was enthusiastic and full of praise for the professional manner in which she had handled everything. And Dirk . . .

The cracks in the wall of her resistance to Dirk suddenly widened. She longed to throw herself down beside Lois and weep. Her whole misunderstanding with him seemed so pointless now, and it could so easily have been remedied if only one of them had been able to act objectively. Instead of wasting the whole miserable day sightseeing in Savannah, why hadn't they thrashed out their problems like two mature adults? Why hadn't they had the courage to probe for whatever emotional thorns were causing them so much pain?

Shane took a shaky breath, aware suddenly that in the endless hours since their quarrel her viewpoint had gradually altered. Now that the shock of Dirk's announcement had worn off, her worst agony wasn't that he had planned to be married. In the past she had often wondered how she had been lucky enough to find him still single. But what rankled now was that he had broken the news to her in such a callous, unfeeling way. What had he said? That he was drifting, that Patrice held out an anchor. There was an emptiness in his life . . . But what kind of man could have hoped to fill it with a woman he claimed not to care for? Not the sensitive, tender man Shane had fallen in love with. She shivered. No, the man who had left his bride in Hong Kong was the same disquieting stranger who had sent her fleeing to the woods to escape his deliberate attempt to hurt her.

Suddenly Shane felt Lois' stare, and she whirled around, her cheeks pink with embarrassment. How long had she been standing there, lost in her own thoughts?

"I'm sorry. I was thinking for a moment of something else."

"Never mind." Lois got to her feet and brushed white speccks of lint from her skit. "I was just commenting on the fact that you're the only scholar on the island. That's unusual, isn't it?"

Shane nodded. "There were five when I arrived. But I was the only one working toward a deadline, so I wasn't included when the others were asked to leave temporarily."

"Asked to leave? I don't understand."

"It seems Dirk found himself with an unexpected block of free time—" Honeymoon time . . . and no one to spend it with. Shane's heart went out to him suddenly. If he was as torn as his behavior indicated, the last thing he needed was a scene like the one that had set them quarreling. Even if he cared nothing for Patrice, as he claimed, calling off a marriage was bound to take a toll. He had needed time to work things through when he came home from Hong Kong, time without the strangers she had insisted he invite. No wonder he had been angry and resentful . . .

Unnerved by the chorus of critics sounding off in her brain, Shane forced herself to focus again on Lois. "Dirk hoped to spend a little time alone on the island. But when he found out that if he asked me to leave I couldn't finish my research in time to take my degree, he let me stay on."

"I see." Lois smiled. "How considerate. And how lucky."

How kind, too, Shane thought. How unselfish and loving and tender, even to a stranger. Shane felt herself consumed with a need to talk to Dirk, to make some kind of amends for the stupid way she had behaved.

But Lois had another question. "You had no idea when you applied for a grant to study here that there might be a Spanish mission on the island?"

Shane tried to hide her agitation at the delay. "No idea at all. I was simply interested in excavating a burial mound with Indian origins."

"Ah—it was fate, then. Your discovery was waiting for you. When can I see it?"

Gratefully Shane went toward the door. "As soon as we've had lunch. Dirk will bring around a Jeep and we'll go and have a look."

Behind her Lois said, "Dirk's been an immeasurable help, hasn't he?"

The tears that had threatened to fall all morning blurred the doorway as Shane passed through. "I don't know what I would have done without him."

The mission site exceeded even the highest hopes of the professor and Lois Traylor. They spent all afternoon and all of the next day inspecting it and the artifacts Dirk and Shane had uncovered.

"It's a spectacular find," exclaimed the jubilant Mitterand the next evening at dinner. "Four hundred years old at least, and up to this point, the first indication ever uncovered that the Spanish settled this far north."

"What I want to know," Frances Forester put in with her usual decisiveness, "is what ended the activity here."

The professor nodded. "The mission development, yes."

"Perhaps we will discover the answer to that," Lois inserted eagerly. "Or it may remain a mystery forever. But the important thing is that it did exist, and for our purpose, the icing on the cake is that it existed in an area of relatively little modern development. In other words, we have the site intact, not like in St. Augustine and other populated areas where the big problem is sifting through a variety of cultures."

James Mitterand raised his wineglass to Shane. "And we owe it all to you, my dear."

Shane flushed. In honor of the occasion she

had worn the same pink silk she had put on the first night she had dined with Dirk. The soft, flickering light at the table cast flattering shadows on the oval countours of her face, highlighting the nervous agitation she felt at not having been able to speak privately with Dirk, even for a few minutes. Now she glanced quickly at him as she answered the professor.

"I can't claim all the credit for the find. There's the tornado to thank initially. And Dirk, of course. If he hadn't insisted that I take one more look, I would have gone back to Texas without discovering anything out of the ordinary."

"When *do* you go back?" Lois questioned.

Shane met Dirk's even gaze. "My grant expires the sixth of May."

"Only a few more days," the professor said. "What a pity. But the picture has changed since your discovery, hasn't it? Won't you be coming back here when the real work begins on the dig?" He turned to Dirk. "You can arrange that, can't you?"

Shane saw the flush starting at Dirk's collar and understood how he must resent the way the professor had taken over since his arrival. At the dig the afternoon before, a particularly upsetting scene had developed, and Shane cringed, remembering her part in it.

After the professor's initial inspection of the mission site, he had started at once to issue orders.

"The whole area will have to be sealed off," he

informed Dirk. "I want barbed-wire fences erected as soon as we leave here, and signs, of course, every two feet, forbidding trespassing."

Dirk stared coldly at him. "That won't be necessary, sir. The natives all know that this part of the island is off-limits at present."

"Knowing it and respecting it are not the same thing."

Dirk eyed him evenly. "On Wanatoka they are the same."

"Nevertheless," the professor replied briskly, "it won't do at all to leave the site unprotected. We can't tell yet exactly what we have here. Even the most minor disturbance could do irreparable damage. Footprints where we don't want them, children digging in the sand." He looked to Shane for verification. "You're a scientist. You at least ought to understand what I'm saying."

"I do, of course"—Shane licked her lips, aware of Dirk's icy stare—"but . . ."

Mitterand's piercing gaze honed in on her. "There *are* children on this island, aren't there?"

"There are fourteen to be exact," Dirk cut in. "And they do as they are told. They have been told to stay away from here, and they will."

Shane felt obliged to act as arbitrator. "The children of this culture are extremely well-behaved, Professor. They aren't exposed to outside influences that sometimes undermine parental authority." She turned to Dirk with a plea for understanding. "But just the same, I think it might be a wise precaution to follow the professor's advice, just in case—"

"Animals dig in the sand, too." Dirk's acid tone caused Lois to turn around and stare. "Shall we pour concrete and build a wall to restrict the razorbacks? After four hundred years that may be a bit tardy, don't you think? Perhaps the best course is to electrify the wire. Then whatever wanders in, we won't be bothered by it but once."

"You're making quite a fuss over nothing," Shane murmured tightly. "Erecting barriers around a site is a routine procedure, not an insult to the natives."

Lois turned to the professor. "Have you met any of the natives, James? They're charming. I'm sure that Dirk's confidence in them is well-founded."

At once Mitterand's attitude mellowed. "No offense meant, Holland. But you can appreciate, I'm sure, the fact that my first allegiance is to the dig."

"Mine is to the island," Dirk replied curtly.

"It's the same thing, isn't it?" Shane asked, acutely aware that she had made a mess of things.

"I'll see that your wire is strung, Professor," Dirk said. "And I can assure you that no damage will be done to the mission site by anyone living on Wanatoka. In return, I shall expect the same kind of regard for the rest of the island from you and from whoever comes here on your authority."

"Fair enough," the professor agreed, and the unpleasant episode ended. But afterward, things remained strained between the two men.

Now, sitting at the dinner table, Shane shrank from the question Mitterand had just directed toward Dirk.

Before he could answer, she spoke up quickly. "It wouldn't be fair for me to ask to come back. There's always a list of scholars waiting to come to Wanatoka, and I've had my turn."

But the archaeologist wasn't to be put off. "Surely this can be viewed as an exceptional case. Don't you agree, Holland?"

With a cold eye, Dirk gazed down the table at Shane. "I can't force anyone to return who doesn't want to."

She spoke out sharply. "It isn't a question of not wanting to. I have my thesis to complete."

Frances Forester put in, "From what I can gather, this project is likely to develop into the find of the decade, at least. Well worth putting off finishing a thesis for, if you ask me."

Shane gritted her teeth to keep from replying that no one had asked her. With as much restraint as she could muster she said, "I might agree if I hadn't incurred some rather large debts financing my education. I can't afford a delay at this point."

Mitterand smiled more kindly. "That's understandable, of course. And you're quite wise, too. The ivory towers are the place for the sort of work ahead of you. Shut yourself up there and

you'll have it done in no time at all." He sipped
from his wineglass. "But that needn't prevent
you from returning later. As an archaeologist,
you couldn't hope for a finer experience than
taking part in a dig of this kind. Fortunately, it
will be fall before anything of real importance
takes place here, and by then, you'll no doubt
have your work completed."

"Fall?" Dirk frowned, his tone making clear
that he had counted on all the disruption being
over by then. "Why the delay?"

Mitterand smiled expansively. "I suspect in
your kind of work new developments move
along rather more speedily than they do in mine.
For one thing," he said pointedly, "we'll have to
secure funding. Money for this sort of venture
doesn't grow on trees. We'll have to organize a
top team and get our gear together for several
months of intensive investigation. Tentatively
I'm setting September first as our return date."

"Oh, splendid," Frances said. "That gives me
plenty of time to call back the fellows who had to
leave at Easter, and an opportunity to rearrange
future grants." Her rare smile beamed out
around the table. "When everything is tended to,
I may take off for Italy for a few weeks. What
would you say to that, Dirk?"

"I say take off for Italy tomorrow if it pleases
you." Abruptly he pushed back his chair. "Coffee
will be served in the library."

Chapter Eleven

In the library there was a great deal of talk and high good humor except from Dirk, who wandered off by himself to inspect a shelf of historical reference books, and from Shane, who could think only of happy evenings when the two of them had sat alone in contentment, separately following their own reading tastes but joined in a closeness that defied separation.

When the conviviality of the group finally turned to yawns, the professor was the first to rise. To Lois he said, "Our plane leaves at seven. I'm turning in now."

Lois smiled at the pointed suggestion that she ought to do the same, and in a few minutes she rose too. When the front door closed behind Frances Forester as well, only Shane remained behind, tensely eyeing Dirk.

"Well." She cleared her throat hopefully. "I'm sure you're relieved that tomorrow everything returns to normal."

Dirk shelved the book he had been examining and turned around. "Everything?"

"The island routine, I mean."

Dirk snorted. "The island routine won't ever be normal again. The children have been squelched to speechlessness, the north shore looks like a war zone—"

"It hasn't been as bad as all that, has it?"

"It has." He glowered. "And I don't look for any improvement. Mitterand is overbearing enough now. Wait until he gets going full swing."

"He's used to running things, that's all."

Dirk's chin jutted out. "So am I. And on my own island, I plan to continue doing so."

"I'm sorry you've been so unhappy."

"Really?" He eyed her coolly. "I wasn't aware that you'd noticed. You and the professor have been so busy patting each other on the back."

"You found Lois pleasant-enough company, I believe."

Dirk's face relaxed suddenly. "That sounds like the comment of a jealous woman."

"It isn't," she answered sharply. "Not at all." She forced a tight little smile. "I found Lois pleasant company myself. I can understand why you enjoy being around her."

"How magnanimous."

Tears stung at Shane's eyelids. "And how unkind of you to say so in that supercilious tone."

He gave her a withering look and walked over to the hearth.

A long moment of silence followed. Then Shane swallowed the lump in her throat and said in a voice bereft of emotion, "I'd like to talk. Are you going to be up for a while?"

It was the first personal overture she had made to him since their quarrel, and she felt almost as if she had taken off her clothes in front of him.

But if Dirk was aware of her distress, he gave no sign. "I'm going out." He took up the fire tongs and gave the dying blaze a poke. "To count alligators."

"Alligators?" She forgot for a moment how disappointed she was. "What on earth for? Why do they need counting?"

"They're an endangered species." He turned around at last. "Though it's difficult to imagine, considering the number that are roaming around."

A shiver ran over her. "Roaming around here?"

Her nervousness brought forth his low chuckle, and she realized with a stab of longing how much she had missed hearing it.

"They're in the bogs," he said in a less-hostile tone. "One has to call them up."

She bit her lip. "How does one do that?"

"First, one gets a lantern—" He broke off abruptly. "You could come and see for yourself."

"No—it's late."

"It's only a little past nine." His dark eyes glinted suddenly with challenge. "You aren't afraid, are you?"

"Why should I be?" She bristled defensively. "Just a few dozen alligators gaping at me in the middle of the night when I've only a lantern to defend myself?"

"I'll be there. I'll defend you."

She dropped her gaze. After a minute he went on quietly, "There's nothing dangerous about it. I started going out to count gators with my father when I was about ten. Of course, in those days no one was thinking much about the environment. There wasn't an agency urging us to do it. We went just because it was exciting." His gaze lingered on her lips. "It was a time we shared that wasn't shared with anyone else."

Sharper than she meant to, she said, "There must have been quite a few opportunities for that kind of experience in a place as isolated as Wanatoka."

"It wasn't so isolated then. There were always the cotton buyers."

Shane pulled in her breath. "Oh, Dirk—I'm sorry."

"Don't be." His reply came across deliberately careless. "That was all so long ago I scarcely remember it."

"You remember your outings with your father."

He looked into the fire. "Those were happy times."

Yes, Shane thought. The happy times we hold on to. The ones that aren't so happy get buried. But they go on hurting still, festering in the dark . . . sometimes forever.

She said suddenly, "Dirk, did you hate your mother when she ran away?"

He turned around, scowling. "I didn't feel anything for her at all."

Shane's breathing stopped. "You said the same thing about Patrice."

"Did I?" He gave an unpleasant laugh. "Maybe that's because they had a lot in common."

"Do you mean— Are you saying that Patrice was unfaithful too?"

His look darkened again. "I'm saying I don't care if she was or not."

Shane sat forward on the edge of her chair. "Is that what you want to think? Or do you really mean it?"

"Whether I do or not," he lashed out suddenly, "it's really none of your business, is it?"

White-faced, Shane came out of her chair and brushed past him. "On that pleasant note, I'll say good night."

"Wait—" He reached out for her. "I'm sorry." He caught hold of her at the door and spun her around, his hands gripping her shoulders. "That was a stupid thing for me to say. Forget it."

"Oh, sure." Tears stood in her eyes. "Just like I'm supposed to forget all the other unhappy moments we've shared."

"We've shared good times, too," he said hoarsely. His fingers bit into her flesh. "Wonderful times no one else could ever have given me."

"Good night, Dirk."

"Don't go, Shane. You wanted to talk."

"I can't talk to you. I don't know who you are anymore." A tear spilled over. "You were so much fun once, so tender and kind—"

His voice throbbed huskily. "I haven't changed."

"I guess you haven't," she choked. "You have me crying again."

He pulled her against him. "Oh, Shane, there needn't be any tears if we stop wasting the precious time we have left."

His arms offered the harbor she was yearning for; when he was like this, he was a bulwark against everything she feared. . . . But "not wasting time" meant lying beside him again while her need for him, which she could barely control in the best of times, took over and dictated what she did with her life.

She loved him. Oh, yes, she loved him . . . every breath he took, every moody glance, even. But a minute ago he had reaffirmed how perilous it was to love him unrestrainedly. He had the power to hurt her too badly. Patrice was only one ghost in his past. How many other women had he tired of and walked away from? Did he even have the capacity to love?

Trembling, she stepped free of his embrace. "We could never take up where we left off."

"We could—if you wanted to."

"Don't pressure me, Dirk."

His voice thickened. "If you feel pressured, maybe it's because time is running out. The sixth of May is almost here."

She turned her face away.

"Shane, there's so much between us that's still unsettled. Come with me tonight." His hands smoothed her arms. "I've missed you, Shane."

I've missed you, too, her heart cried out. But if she gave in to its clamorings and let him go on hurting her whenever it pleased him, would she be able to pick up the pieces later and carry on with her life? She stared up at him while the moment stretched out. If she couldn't, did it matter?

"Come as a friend, if you want," he urged huskily. "Aren't we still friends, at least?"

"I don't know." Her voice fell to a whisper. "I don't know what we are."

"I can show you." He put out his hand and touched her wet cheek. "I'll wait while you go and change your clothes."

Chapter Twelve

Shane had never been so deep in the woods before. There was no moon, and only by the light of Dirk's lantern was she able to see that they were leaving behind the trails she was familiar with.

"How much farther is it?" she asked shakily when they had tramped for a quarter of an hour.

Dirk lifted a drapery of vines and held it aside for her to pass by. "We're here."

Ahead of them lay an inky pool. Rotting tree trunks towered from its murkiness. Shane glanced around, terrified all at once.

"Don't be afraid." He gave her hand a reasuring squeeze. Then he walked away and hung the lantern on a limb as high above him as he could reach.

When he came back, he whispered, "Watch."

For a few minutes Shane could see no change in the syrupy-looking water. Then, like small glowing embers, two red eyes popped up on its surface. To the right two more appeared. In a moment they were gleaming everywhere.

Shane grabbed for Dirk's wrist.

"Count," he murmured.

"I don't know where to start."

"Use the tree stumps as points of reference."

A faintly hysterical giggle lodged in her throat. "Do I divide by two?"

Dirk rasped, "Thirteen, fourteen. Count!"

After half an hour they moved on to more distant ponds. By the time they reached the third one Shane was totally absorbed in what she was doing.

"They're best tallied in zigzags," she informed Dirk in the tone she often used at the dig.

"Are they really?" he replied. "Thanks for the tip." But he smiled as he watched her slender form striking out confidently toward the pond's bank.

It was long past midnight when they came back to the welcome fire in the library. While Dirk poured fingers of brandy for each of them, Shane slipped out of her boots and warmed herself in front of the comforting glow on the hearth.

Still intent on comparing the grubby slips of paper on which each of them had recorded their count, she took the snifter he handed her without looking up. "It averages out to two hundred and sixty-seven." She gave a low, satisfied whistle. "No gator shortage here. I guess the environmental agency will be glad to hear that."

The leather chair Dirk slid into received him

with a sigh. "Actually the daytime count is the one we'll report."

Her glance flew up. "What daytime count?"

"The one Kimbo will make in the morning."

"Do you mean that we've been stomping around out there for hours for nothing?"

"Not exactly." He smiled at her outraged look. "It's always fun to see how many of the old fellows the lantern can draw up."

"Fun!"

"Wasn't it fun?" His steady look dared her to deny the feeling of closeness and contentment that had been rekindled between them as they walked along holding hands in the black night.

"Well," she answered lamely, "I can think of more pleasurable ways to spend an evening."

"So can I." He fixed his luminous gaze on her. "But they're off-limits for friends."

Shane turned her face toward the fire.

After a minute he said, "Why did you stay behind tonight after the others went to bed?"

"I told you." Shane swallowed. "I wanted to talk."

"Do you still want to?"

She brought her gaze around. "Do you want to listen?"

"Yes."

She chewed her lip, uncertain now if it was worth going into. Tramping through the bogs, they had reestablished enough of their old rapport to allow her to hope that in a day or two everything might be all right again.

Dirk broke into her thoughts. "If you have something to say, say it. I promise not to eat you."

Once he had wanted to, she recalled. Once he could never have sat for this long so far away from her, gazing at her in that luminous, heated way without touching her. Her yearning for him was suddenly so great that she found herself gulping for breath.

"In Savannah," she began haltingly, "when we—when you were discussing your relationship with Patrice—I don't think I gave you quite a fair hearing."

Dirk watched her for a moment. "It seemed to me you heard more than you wanted to."

"I heard something unexpected." A rush of blood came to her cheeks. "I wasn't prepared for what you told me. Afterward I realized that I reacted badly.

Then, because she felt he must know how hard this was for her and he wasn't helping, she added in a bristly tone, "I do think you might have picked a better time to talk about your past amours."

"One amour." He got out of his chair. At the hearth he stirred the logs, and a stream of sparks flew up. "What's the point in bringing all this up again?"

"If it's going to upset you, forget it. I only mentioned it because I've been wondering if my behavior prevented you from saying all you wanted to say that day."

He turned around and stared directly at her.

"If you feel guilty, it ought to be because you're leaving when you could stay on until I leave in June."

"I don't feel guilty! I never agreed to doing that—but even if I had, I wouldn't now. Everything is different between us."

"It wasn't different tonight."

"We managed a truce. We spent a few pleasant hours together. But we haven't dealt with any of the real issues that are dividing us. I'm not sure we ever can."

"We can't if you go running off."

"Dirk, you haven't listened to me. I have responsibilities. I can't just dump them."

"You could relax and enjoy what each day offers without thinking the fate of the world hinges on whether or not you do your duty."

The pat way he viewed her problems enraged her. "I'm not like you. I've never had the money or the freedom money gives to do just as I pleased. I've had to borrow and scrimp and plan every detail of my life. I've never been at liberty to act on whims."

"Maybe it's time you started."

"You've known all along what I'm like. By necessity I'm practical and determined and economical. I set goals for myself and I achieve them. That's the way I'm structured. I can't change."

"But you expect me to change."

"What?" Her heart took a sudden leap. "What do you mean?"

He gazed intently at her. "What you're angling for from me, what you've wanted all along is a positive commitment, isn't it? You want me to say, Marry me, Shane. And then everything will be all right."

"I am not angling for anything." She fought against her breathlessness. "But if you're going to go on insisting I stay here, I think I have a right to know how you feel about me and what you see in the future for us."

"I don't have a crystal ball. But if I say I love you, will that make everything right? Will you throw your goals out the window and settle in here for as long as I want?"

"You're cruel."

"So are you, putting a fence around me—do this or else."

Shane's face turned chalky. "You're deliberately misinterpreting everything I've said."

"What I'm doing is telling you what *I'm* like. I haven't said I love you because I don't know if I do. I've never been on speaking terms with love. My one experience with marriage aborted before it even got off the ground." He took a sudden step toward her and pulled her up out of her chair, into his arms. "But I do care about you, Shane." His voice roughened. "No other person on earth could have persuaded me to let a man like Mitterand come here and give me orders. When I'm with you, all kinds of things seem possible that never did before. I don't know yet if I have the capacity to give love. I don't know if what I feel will last. I have to have time to find out. That's the way *I'm* structured. Don't expect change from me when you don't demand it of yourself."

The silence in the room was suddenly deafening. Shane licked her parched lips. When she had her breath back again, she said in a small, tight voice, "What *can* I expect from you?"

"Everything I can possibly give you." His look softened. "In time, maybe a very great deal. Or maybe nothing but good-bye. Will you take a chance?"

Shane swallowed.

"If you won't stay until June, will you meet me back here again in the fall when the work begins again on the dig?"

"I've already told you, I won't be free in the fall." He was asking too much. She had already known more pain from him than she could bear. "I've worked too hard and too long to earn a teaching fellowship. I can't afford to pass it up."

"Delay it, then, just for a year."

Shane fought her desire to give in. "The time to move ahead in my field is now, not a year from now."

"How could you get ahead in your field any faster than taking part in the most exciting excavation of the decade?"

She answered tightly, "People are depending on me. They've loaned me money."

"If money is all that's holding you back, I'll give you whatever you want."

She struggled in his arms, but he held her fast, ignoring her prideful protests. "We've found something more precious than the mission site or your degree or anything else that either of us has ever encountered. Give it a chance, Shane, to become whatever it can be. Don't walk out on it now."

Her voice shook. "If what we've found is love, it will endure whether we're together or not."

"You can't really believe that. Love needs to be nurtured."

"Are you an authority suddenly? A moment ago you knew nothing about love."

He took his arms away. "You don't want to be convinced, do you?"

"I don't want to be persuaded into a decision I may regret for the rest of my life."

"Don't blame me for that. That may be exactly what you're doing to yourself with your damned rigid plans and your one-way view of how your life ought to be run."

The disgust in his voice moved her as nothing else had. Rashly she blurted out, "If I do agree to come back in the fall—I'm not saying that I will—but if I promise to seriously consider it, will you make a promise to me?"

"What is it?"

"Will you contact Indigo?"

"Indigo! Why?"

Panicked, she wondered herself. Intuition? Impulse? But she was in too far to back out. "It just seems to me that something is blocking your feelings. The events of the past. A fixation. Indigo had the same experiences as you. Maybe talking to each other would help."

"Oh, I see." His lips twisted in a bitter smile. "You're taking up psychology now, probing the secret torments of the soul instead of Indian burial mounds."

Her chin trembled. "You're all for having *me* change *my* plans! But when something is required of you, you want no part of it."

"Indigo has been out of my life since I was ten. She has nothing to do with you and me, or with who I am now."

"I think you're wrong."

"Shall I look up my mother too?" he lashed out. "And how about Patrice?"

His acid tone scalded her, but she doggedly pursued her point. "Look up whoever you have to. But if you won't, I don't see any way we can patch up our differences."

He stared down at her. Finally he said grudgingly, "What if I contact Indigo and she refuses to talk to me?"

Shane trembled with hope. "Then we'll go from there."

"I don't know what happened to my mother. She may be dead."

"Surely Indigo will know."

He raised his eyes slowly. "You drive a mean bargain."

"Not mean, Dirk."

"I'll have to think about it."

Suddenly she was angry again. "You have the whole summer."

He gazed steadily at her. "How do you suggest I handle the next ten days?"

Her poise slipped and she blazed out, "You could bury your head in the sand."

A surprising grin turned up his lips. "Or I could spend every minute of it with you, trying to make up my mind."

"Suit yourself."

"I will." But when she turned away abruptly, he reached out and stopped her from going into the hallway. "Will you ride with me in the morning?"

"Oh, Dirk—" All at once she went limp in his arms. "Why do you want me to?"

"I don't know why I want you to. That's what I'm trying to find out." He brushed away a tear that she wasn't able to blink back fast enough. "Will you help me? Will you meet me at the stables at six?"

Six. Only a few hours away. A great hunger to lie down beside him until then surged over her. What a long, terrible time it had been since she had known the warm sliding of his flesh on hers . . . his arms encircling her . . . his lips kissing away every troublesome thought. . . .

"Shane?"

"Yes—" The whisper forced itself through a throat tight with yearning. "I'll be there at six."

Chapter Thirteen

❧

The same blue-and-white Cessna that had brought Dirk to Wanatoka arrived at a few minutes past seven for the professor and Lois. Dirk and Shane got down off their horses to say good-bye.

"It's been a fascinating experience to be on your island, Holland." The professor put out his hand. "I look forward to coming back."

"So do I," Lois said. Her skin had tanned in the hours she had spent inspecting the dig. Watching her chat animatedly with Dirk, Shane realized that if she decided against returning to the island in the fall, it wasn't inconceivable that Lois and he might have an affair.

"And you, my dear Shane?" Shane glanced up to find Professor Mitterand's gray eyes probing hers. "Are you sure you can't be won over?"

She blinked, startled. Had he read her mind? "I'm sorry," she murmured. "I'm afraid I wasn't listening."

Lois' tinkling laughter sounded. "Shane has a way of drifting off from time to time. Woolgathering is what my mother used to call it. The academic term is creative meditation, I believe."

Dirk spoke up. "The professor was reiterating his suggestion from last night at dinner—that you join them again in the fall."

Mitterand said, "Being in on something like this is a chance in a lifetime. Remember, the classroom will always be waiting."

"Do consider coming back," Lois urged with a friendly smile. But Shane noticed that she stayed close to Dirk, and when the Cessna lifted off the sand a few minutes later, Shane imagined that Lois' wave of farewell was directed only at him.

As soon as the plane had disappeared, Dirk turned to Shane with the suggestion that they ride across the island for a look at the dig.

"It's time for breakfast," Shane answered, still smarting from the left-out feeling seeing Lois and Dirk together had given her.

Looking annoyingly relaxed, Dirk grinned. "Why do you always think of food before anything else?"

"I was thinking of Juno! No one else ever seems to."

"Meaning me?" Dirk mounted his horse again. "What's upset you?"

"What makes you think anything has? Just because I care that your cook might be inconvenienced if we don't show up on time? It's not unreasonable, is it, to care about another human being's feelings?"

The mare, sensitive to the tension in the air,

danced away from her, and Shane had to make a grab for the reins before she could swing up in the saddle.

"Actually," Dirk retaliated mildly, "I was judging by the color of your face. It's turkey red."

"Compared to Lois' buttery tan, I guess anyone would look like a turkey." Shane longed for the release a good cry could bring. The morning was extraordinarily beautiful. Clouds had pulled a lavender scarf over the sunrise. For once the waves were still. The songs of birds floated lightly toward them. There would be mornings like this on Wanatoka forever. Would she be here to see them?

"I may have a fever," she told Dirk curtly. "Mosquitoes are everywhere."

"Do you know what you remind me of?" He rode along beside her, wearing an amused smile. "You're just like you were that evening when you came in from your burial mound and I told you there wasn't any water for a bath."

Shane stared straight ahead. "That's a perfect example of your warped sense of humor."

"Which is better than not having any sense of humor at all. You're jealous of Lois, aren't you?"

"Of course not."

"There's certainly no need for you to be. Maybe it's something out of your deep dark past. A fixation that you ought to investigate."

Shane swung around angrily. "Why do you keep throwing rocks at me?"

"Because I hope you'll explode," he answered smoothly. "Then maybe I'll find out what's really going on in that beautiful head of yours."

"I'm tired, that's all."

"You were fine earlier."

"I think it's pointless riding all the way over to the dig when it's sealed off."

"It isn't yet." Pulling in his horse, he let her pass ahead through the narrow opening in the undergrowth. When they were both on the other side, he said, "I told Kimbo to hold off putting up the barriers until you'd had a chance to have a last private look."

"Oh." Shane bit her lip. "I see. That was thoughtful."

"Ah—that's more like it. Now you're sounding like yourself," he murmured. "Like my Shane."

Her color deepened. "But I'm not your Shane. So please don't call me that."

He smiled, amused. "Not even for old times' sake?"

"Not for any reason. Not at this point."

"It's by your own choice that you're going away, you know."

"And it's your choice that you're not!"

He turned in his saddle. "So that's what's eating you—in September Lois will be here and you won't. You have only your stubbornness to blame for that."

"We discussed all of this quite thoroughly last night."

"Not thoroughly enough if you think I give a

damn about Lois Traylor." He caught hold of the mare's reins and pulled both their horses to a stop under the spreading shade of an oak. "You can't forget, can you, that I was almost married. I told you about Patrice and that's when everything good between us ended."

Shane's lips quivered. "We were in trouble before that."

"Trouble? That isn't how I'd describe what we had."

"Then you've forgotten the things you said to me that day in the library."

"And you've forgotten that you pardoned me." His dark eyes glittered with challenge. "I spoke out of childish anger and you graciously forgave me."

Shane pulled herself erect. "I'm not going to sit here and be chewed to death by insects while you reminisce. Are we going to the dig or not?"

Dirk pressed his knees into the stallion's belly. "Lead the way."

As Shane and Dirk approached the oak where they had first discovered the Spanish relics, a new sense of desolation swept over her. Already the dig site had changed. The professor and Lois had staked off the area to be sealed against trespassers. Kimbo and his crew had brought in materials for erecting an equipment shed and a barbed-wire fence. The privacy she and Dirk had once shared was destroyed. It was no longer their domain, and it was hard to imagine as she got down off her horse and stood looking around that this was the same spot where Dirk had introduced her to the rapture of his lovemaking.

Dirk read her dismay in the slump of her shoulders, and after he had tethered the horses, he came back to her side. "Can you see now why I wanted to keep strangers away?"

She only nodded, her throat too full to answer. The ride had cooled her temper, and now all she could think of was the enormous loss that was facing her. Dirk, the island, the dig . . . a whole way of life that would never be hers again.

"Poor little Shane," Dirk murmured at her side. "You make things so hard for yourself."

"Don't pity me," she choked.

Catching hold of her shoulders, he turned her gently toward him. "I don't. I admire you. More than you'll ever know."

His lips moved in her hair. "Maybe you can forget what we found here, but I can't."

She murmured feebly, "I asked you not to pressure me."

"In a few days you'll be gone. That's a pressure I'm not responsible for. I can't help resisting it."

He brought his lips to her mouth, but before they met, Shane felt him tense. He stepped back, letting her go.

"There's a plane coming in."

Shane heard it too, a light whirring close to the shore on the other side of the island. "Somebody on the Cessna must have left something behind."

Dirk's voice lost its warmth. "The efficient professor would never allow that to happen." He started toward the horses. "That's not the Cessna's engine anyway."

They crossed the island in a gallop, but before they reached the opposite shore, the plane that had come in took off again, circling once above them in the strangely still air and then disappearing into the bank of clouds that had risen in the east.

Shane felt an odd stirring in the pit of her stomach. "If they dropped somebody off, who could it be?"

Ahead of her, Dirk answered grimly, "Who else but the second wave of the invasion."

"A dig team?" Shane gasped. "Not already. That's impossible."

"How about a press team?"

"They couldn't know either. Not yet."

"Couldn't they?" The horses brought Shane and Dirk out of the undergrowth onto the beach. "Look at that."

Coming across the sand toward them were two men carrying cameras and a woman hanging on to a large leather bag slung over one shoulder.

The man in the lead called out, "Are you Dirk Holland?"

Dirk reined in beside him. "Who are you?"

"I'm Baxter Lindsay of the Miami *News-Herald*." He nodded across his shoulder at the man beside him. "This is Bill Porter of KLVN-TV out of St. Augustine."

The woman, a slim, striking brunette, stepped forward with her own introduction. "I'm Karen

Phillips, Mr. Holland. *Women in the News* is my magazine." She turned with businesslike briskness to Shane. "I'm here to do a profile on Shane McBride. If you're she and if what I've been told is true, you have a startling story to tell. *WIN* is willing to pay handsomely for it."

Dirk cut in abruptly. "Who invited you here?"

The man from St. Augustine answered crisply, "The press doesn't wait for invitations, Mr. Holland. We cover the news wherever it's happening."

Dirk thundered, "Not on my island! Get off!"

No one moved. The man called Baxter Lindsay eyed him evenly. "We understand that the remains of a four-hundred-year-old Spanish mission have been discovered on this island, Mr. Holland. I'm sure you wouldn't want to deprive the public of the interesting facts concerning this find, would you?"

"I would if I chose to."

Shane found her voice at last. "At the moment there's nothing to disclose." She had assured Dirk; she had asked him to trust her in regard to the press. "In a few more months—"

"In a few more months," Karen Phillips put in smoothly, "every branch of the media will know what's happening here." She shifted her smile to Dirk's grim face. "We've sniffed out a story before anyone else. We've gone to quite a lot of trouble to get here. Don't you think we at least deserve a look at your beautiful island?"

"We have a series in mind," Bill Porter interjected.

Dirk clenched his teeth. "There won't be any series."

"Dirk—"

"I'll handle this, Shane."

Karen Phillips pressed forward. "So *you* are Shane McBride." With a slender hand she caressed the mare's mane. "Do you always ride to the mission site? Or is it within walking distance?"

"It's on the opposite side of the island," Shane answered before she could stop herself.

Dirk glared. "We are not conducting a press conference."

"The press is here," Bill Porter quipped. "We'll be glad to oblige."

"I'm afraid there won't be time," Dirk told him curtly. "You have a long swim ahead of you."

Karen Phillips pulled a notebook and pen out of her satchel. "That's an interesting remark, Mr. Holland. Heartless, one might say." Smiling, she flipped to a clean white page. "Are you generally regarded as a cruel man?"

"Of course he isn't cruel," Shane burst out, and then wished she could bite her tongue off when she saw Dirk's angry flush. With her own cheeks flaming, she added hotly, "Who informed you about the mission site?"

"That's rather obvious, isn't it?" Dirk cut her down with his look. "Selling a story to a magazine is a handy way to retire one's debts."

Karen Phillips watched the color leave Shane's face. Pen poised over her paper, she inquired pleasantly, "Is there something about your discovery that might cause difficulties for you and Mr. Holland if the public finds out about it?"

Shane struggled to regain her composure. "Certainly not."

Baxter Lindsay put in mildly, "Despite your suggestion, Mr. Holland, we won't be leaving until our plane returns at the next low tide." He paused to let the group gathered on the sand listen to the threatening rumble of thunder emitting from the clouds. "It seems to me the civilized thing to do would be to adjourn to the Foundation Center before we all get drenched."

Dirk responded bitingly, "Civilization is twenty miles in the direction you came from. Wanatoka, as you obviously were not informed, is a primitive island."

"Oh, I see." Lindsay returned Dirk's angry glower with a look of calm detachment. "That sounds as if the report that you keep slaves here might be true."

"Get off my property," Dirk commanded.

Scribbling furiously, Karen commented, "Since none of us can walk on water, I'd say you've just made the second threat against our lives, Mr. Holland."

Shane moistened her lips. "Dirk—" There would be time later to confront him about the brutal remark he had made concerning her part in this fiasco. In the meantime someone had to do something to stop it from worsening. "Mr. Lindsay is right. We're going to drown out here in a minute. Can't we please go to the house and sort this out to everyone's satisfaction?"

Instead of an answer, Dirk settled a long, contemptuous stare on her. Then, digging his heels into the stallion's sides, he galloped off through the undergrowth.

Shane turned back to the waiting trio. In a voice void of emotion she said, "The Center is only a short walk from here. If you'll follow me, I'll show you the way."

Chapter Fourteen

The three representatives of the press remained on Wanatoka until nearly noon when a helicopter, hastily summoned by Frances Forester, swooped down on the lawn and spirited them off again toward the mainland.

When the clattering of its propeller had died away, Frances turned to Shane. "Well, you're quite a remarkable young lady."

Oblivious to the rare compliment, Shane turned her anxious gaze back toward the mansion. "You would have handled it much better than I if you'd had any warning."

"That's true," Frances replied with her customary lack of modesty. "But, remember, I've been in the public eye for quite a number of years. You're only a student."

"I feel like a veteran of the Hundred Years' War at the moment. I can understand now why people who have to deal regularly with the press hire agents to do it for them."

Frances' gaze warmed once again. "You showed a great deal of insight, I thought—

ushering those people into the solarium and treating them like a trio of hothouse flowers. Tea and scones." She chuckled. "And served by one of the island's 'slaves.' It was utterly delightful."

"It's over. That's the main thing."

Frances squinted up at the rain-washed sky. "Imagine the nerve of them, dropping down on us like that. Terribly nosy fellows, too, though neither of them compared with that girl for prying out information. What was the name of her magazine?"

"*WIN, Women in the News.* What do you suppose has become of Dirk? He was livid when I last saw him."

Frances started with her toward the veranda. "Wanatoka is sacred ground to Dirk. Or haven't you noticed?"

"Oh, Frances—" In the last couple of hours Shane had stopped caring about formalities or what the older woman might think of her. The harrying time they had spent fending off their uninvited guests had made them allies of a sort. All Shane really cared about now was reassuring herself that nothing that had been said would reflect unfavorably on Dirk or on Wanatoka. "Do you think Lindsay and the others were convinced that the natives have good lives here?" She shuddered, remembering Baxter Lindsay's jibe about slavery.

"If they aren't convinced," Frances responded confidently, "they're fools. They saw Juno in command of the kitchen, didn't they? And

Saphirra made quite a nice impression, too, relating her family's history in that lovely, sincere way she has." Stepping up onto the porch, Frances added thoughtfully, "But you might have done better asking Kimbo's wife, Faymora, to come and talk to them. She has a degree from Emory University, you know, and speaks three languages. I would have enjoyed seeing her set that Phillips person on her ear."

Shane leaned wearily against a brick column. "When Bill Porter began questioning Saphirra, it seemed best just to let it develop without any prompting from me."

Frances nodded vigorously. "It all went off beautifully. We got rid of them, and they weren't allowed to trample on the site or even set eyes on it." She put her hands on her stocky hips in the way that had cowed even Baxter Lindsay when he had suggested a tour of the island. "But I must admit that I've rather enjoyed all the coming and going of the past few days. It would have been a dull spring without it."

"It's too bad Dirk doesn't share that opinion," Shane answered glumly.

"He may come around eventually. At any rate he's changed since you arrived."

"Has he?" Startled, Shane came to attention. "In what way?"

"In surprising ways." All at once Frances was her formidable self again. "In ways I don't choose to discuss. I have been associated with the Holland family for thirty-five years, and I have never carried tales. If you want to know about Dirk, ask Dirk."

She marched across the veranda and opened the front door. "I'm going in for my lunch now, and I'd advise you to do the same. You've been as pale as a ghost all morning. I shouldn't be at all surprised if you weren't in need of an iron injection."

Despite Frances Forester's dour assessment of the state of her health, Shane skipped lunch in favor of saddling the mare again and riding off across the island in search of Dirk. His remark about her having tipped off the reporters in the hope of making money out of it still stung, but she was able now to recognize it for what it was— merely an angry reaction. Dirk knew she had no way of contacting the mainland. Furthermore, now that more urgent matters had made the incident seem silly, she found it hard to believe that Dirk really held such a low opinion of her. At any rate, she was anxious to confront him.

But he was not to be found in any of the places where she looked. The alligator ponds were murky and still. Along the forest paths only small, burrowing animals stirred. When she reached the mission site, it appeared depressingly forlorn too.

Since early morning when she had visited it with Dirk, the perimeters of the dig had been cordoned off with barbed wire, and forbidding signs were posted every few feet—as if the rabbits and the wild turkeys could read.

Deflated, she got down off her horse for the look-around that had been cut short by the arrival of the plane. But before she could loop the reins around one of the fence posts, she heard the familiar snort of the stallion and saw, as she turned, the horse with Dirk astride it emerging from a nearby thicket.

Relief welled up in her and she called out jokingly, "So there you are. I'd almost decided you'd taken your own advice and swum toward the mainland."

Dirk eyed her without a flicker of amusement. "I heard the helicopter. Are they gone?"

"Yes—" Resentment crowded her throat. "No thanks to you."

"I didn't invite them to come here."

"Neither did I—no matter what you think."

"You may not have mailed out engraved invitations, but you're responsible just the same for that disgusting exhibition of arrogance on the beach."

Shane sucked in her breath. "The reporters weren't alone in their arrogance."

"I don't have to apologize for anything I said. This island happens to belong to me."

"As if we haven't all heard that ten thousand times."

"What was it *you* said? 'Trust me,' wasn't that it? 'And it will all work out.'" Dirk scowled contemptuously. "Now we know how."

"You don't know how!" Shane trembled with rage. "Because you weren't man enough to stay around and see. If Frances hadn't come to my rescue, and if Juno and Saphirra hadn't stuck by me like troopers, heaven knows what would have happened. We certainly could have used a little support from the island's owner. But, no, he was off sulking in the bushes."

Dirk swung down off his horse. "In the bushes! I was here at this damned site all morning stringing up wire and posting the professor's pretty little signs before your friends came swarming over everything and tore it to pieces."

Shane blinked. "You were here? But I thought Kimbo—"

"Kimbo is working on the other side of the island at the washout. He had instructions not to touch anything here until you'd said your last good-byes—" Dirk's glare bored into her. "Or don't you remember my mentioning that before your buddies from the media dropped in on us?"

"They are not my buddies!" Shane swallowed a throatful of tears. "But I'll tell you one thing: if you care about Wanatoka, you won't antagonize the press. I did what I could today to patch up the harm your belligerence caused. But the next time it happens I won't be here."

"Is that some kind of threat?"

"I'm just warning you."

"I don't need your warnings," he cut in acidly. "There's never going to be a repetition of what happened here today."

"You're burying your head in the sand again. You can't keep Wanatoka isolated forever."

"No, I can't." His bitter gaze swept over her. "That's something I owe to you. But I'm taking care of that. After today nobody's going to set foot on this island without cleared credentials."

Shane's voice shook. "I think that's an excellent idea. You should have thought of it a month ago—and you might have, if you hadn't been so obsessed with preserving the past that you couldn't evaluate the present."

"And how, in your humble opinion, could I have handled things better?"

"You could have faced up to the way the world has changed since you were ten years old." Her eyes glittered with unshed tears. "You could have recognized the bias that's crippling you. The enemy isn't out there, Dirk, wearing Shangri-la perfume and falling in love with cotton buyers. The enemy is inside you. You're so afraid your precious prejudices will be invaded, you've strung barbed wire all around yourself and your island too. I hope today proved that it won't work—that it never has."

"What today proved is that you don't love this island the way you claimed." He stared down at her, ashen-faced and with steel in his eyes. "You don't love me either. All you care about is yourself and being right. You told me once when you set a goal you always reach it—no matter what. But I never really believed you meant it until I saw you today on the beach buttering up those reporters."

Shane blanched. "I was trying to save your silly neck!"

"You were trying to get your name in the paper."

Shane pushed past him toward her horse. But even when she was astride it and pounding down the path toward the mansion, his taunting words still rang in her ears.

Chapter Fifteen

Shane climbed out of the taxi in front of the university library and fumbled nervously in her purse for money to pay the driver.

He smiled, glancing approvingly at her trim figure sleekly outlined in an expensive pink gown. Lois Traylor had sent her the gown from New York for this particular evening, which Shane thought of wryly as her debut.

"It's a big night for you, isn't it?" the driver observed as she handed across her fare. Then a little bashfully he added, "I saw your picture in the paper this morning."

The August sun that had baked the campus all day had finally slipped behind the Texas hills, but stored-up heat still rose from the sidewalk, and as the driver made his comment, Shane felt its warmth mingling with the heat of her embarrassment. Over the past few weeks, since news of the mission site had been publicized, trying to accustom herself to being recognized by strangers was the most difficult adjustment she had ever faced. Except one.

Once more—as had been happening all summer—she thought of that May evening that was still so painfully engraved in her memory: Frances and Saphirra waving good-bye as the helicopter lifted off the lawn again, and in the distance Dirk—still in the clothes he had worn at the dig—visible through an open window, having his dinner alone. . . .

"Your change, ma'am."

Shane jumped. "Oh, keep it."

The driver smiled. "Nervous?" He made a circle of his forefinger and thumb. "Don't worry. You look like a million dollars. You'll knock 'em dead in there."

"Thanks." Shane waved as he drove away. "Thanks very much. I needed that."

This kickoff reception at Shane's alma mater was the first in a series planned at universities around the country in the hope of raising sufficient funds to excavate the mission site on Wanatoka. It was the only one she had agreed to attend. But as she entered the elegant faculty reception room, panic knotted her stomach. She knew it would take more than a cabbie's good wishes to get her through this evening.

A handful of early arrivals had gathered in the center of the room to chat. In their midst stood Dirksen Holland.

Until yesterday she had been sure he wouldn't show up. The university had pulled out all stops to make the reception the kind of occasion the national media would take notice of, and Professor Mitterand had never let up in his insistence that both discoverers of the silver medallion be present.

Shane had counted on Dirk's aversion to publicity to keep him away. For weeks the papers had been panning him for the way he shunned the press and for the tight security he had wrapped around Wanatoka. She had grown used to the unflattering pictures they printed of him. Looking at his grim face glaring into the eye of the camera had helped, in fact, in her daily battle to get him out of her life. Who could care for anyone so obviously obsessed with his possessions? He would be the last person on earth to lend support to a cause destined to change his beloved island.

Then, the evening before, just as she was finally relaxing enough to look forward a little to the occasion, Lois Traylor had telephoned with the "good news" that Dirk had relented. He had decided to fly to Texas and attend the reception after all.

Shane's first thought had been to run. Learning to live without Dirk during the long days of summer had been as debilitating as a major illness. She still wasn't over feeling shaky each time she saw a man on the street who walked in the same easy way as Dirk did or whose head was topped with similar swirls of dark, unruly hair.

Hanging up from Lois' call, she made up her mind to go home for a visit. She had even gone as far as dialing the airline, asking about reservations.

Now, as Dirk turned and caught sight of her trembling in her pink crepe de chine, she wished she had carried through with that childish urge to flee. The same overwhelming rush of love she had experienced on Wanatoka gripped her. Nothing had changed. Those long, painful months of renouncing him might never have happened. Watching him walk toward her, she felt as if she had left his arms only yesterday . . . as if the imprint of his mouth on hers was still there, throbbing with promise. . . .

"Shane—" He stopped in front of her, towering and virile. "Hello."

"Dirk." Fire rippled over her skin at his touch. "How are you?"

"About as you'd expect, I imagine." His half-smile lit his craggy face. "Not quite comfortable in this situation, but better now that you're here."

She swallowed. "I'm surprised to see you."

"No one told you I was coming?"

"Yes, I knew." All the restless nights she had spent telling herself she despised him, all the vows she had made never to think of him again . . . It was all wasted time now that he was here beside her. His voice, those indigo eyes touching every part of her . . . "Lois telephoned with the news. But knowing how you feel about this sort of thing, I thought you might back out."

"I couldn't chance giving Mitterand a stroke. Anyway"—another slow smile started on his lips—"if you can't beat 'em, doesn't the old adage advise that you join 'em?"

Shane's mouth had gone dry as powder. "It's hard to imagine your being influenced by tired old maxims."

"Maybe I've reformed." His eyes took on a brilliant glitter. "There was room for improvement, wouldn't you say?"

Flustered, she answered with a touch of sarcasm, "You're being unusually agreeable. Any special reason?"

He lowered his voice. "A whole roomful of reasons. And at the moment every one of them is looking at us."

Shane swung around. Then froze. The reception hall had filled as they talked, and now, as Dirk had said, all eyes were trained on the handsome couple by the door.

Shane gripped Dirk's arm at her side. "Why are they staring? What's expected of us?"

Dirk's comforting hand tightened at her waist. "All that's expected is for us to smile," he murmured beneath his own smile. "And to make pleasant, informative conversation so that, when the evening is over, they'll go home feeling as if the hundred dollars they paid to come here wasn't quite enough."

Shane still held back, clutching his arm with icy fingers.

"Don't be afraid. You may not know their names, but they're friends, or they wouldn't be here. They support your cause." Holding her firmly at his side, he began to move forward. "Just be yourself. Let them know you appreciate their help. That's all there is to it."

Shane was soon separated from him. The crowd pressed around, and she saw him drifting off, surrounded by individuals eager to have a word with the notorious Dirksen Holland before the night was over. Friends, she kept reminding herself when her face began to ache from smiling. And many of them, she admitted as the evening wore on, did seem like people she knew and loved in her own home town.

Then at last the guests began to trickle away. Dirk joined Shane at the refreshment table while the host for the evening poured champagne for them and proclaimed his pleasure at how well things had gone.

"What a tremendous success! Fifty additional subscriptions in excess of the presale. And all due, I'm certain, to your being here." His beaming gaze swept over the two of them. "There's nothing like the excitement of having the principals present. Personally, I could listen half a dozen more times to your account of pulling the first medallion out of the sand. Fantastic!"

Finally they were able to say good night. Dirk walked with Shane out to the library steps.

"Exhausted?" he inquired when they were alone.

"Yes." She managed one more smile. "But exhilarated too. Actually, it was fun. As you said, there were so many nice people—"

He broke in quietly. "May I see you home?"

All evening she had dreaded this moment. Afraid he would ask. Afraid he wouldn't. "It isn't necessary, Dirk. Really, it isn't."

"That wasn't my question."

While he hailed a taxi, she tried to remember how she had left the apartment. Were there still lunch dishes on the kitchen counter? Had she strewn her clothes about in the bedroom?

But when Dirk unlocked the door and they stepped inside, everything was in order, as it always was. A fresh bouquet of bluebells stood in a glass vase on the coffee table. In the corner a lamp shed a soft light over her desk and the books stacked there in tidy piles. Nothing in the inviting atmosphere of her quarters revealed in any way that within these walls she had suffered.

Dirk looked around with an appreciative smile. "I pictured you in a setting like this. I'm glad you let me come here."

She moved quickly toward the kitchen. "Can I get you a drink? Soda may be all I have—"

"Shane." He turned around. "Could we talk instead?" He saw her hesitate, and he came toward her, pausing next to her in the tiny alcove that served as a kitchen and barely afforded room for one. "There are things I'd like to tell you."

"There are things I'd like to tell you, too," she said. He stood so close that she could feel his warmth reaching out to her. "One is thank you—for getting me through this evening."

"You did that yourself with your naturalness and your smile." His gaze caressed her. Or was she imagining that? "I always remember how you smiled at me the day I landed on Wanatoka." He chuckled softly. "The perfect hostess, offering me a ride on my own horse."

Her smiled trembled and she wondered if beneath the soft cloth that covered her breast he could see her heart pounding. "I felt like such a fool when I found out who you were."

"You didn't act like a fool. You went off like a firecracker, as I recall. Railing at me for my chauvinistic tendencies."

"That wasn't fair," she said faintly. The scent of his skin had reached her nostrils. She remembered in vivid detail the shape of his body next to hers, the power of his kiss.

"Maybe it *was* fair. I don't remember that man very well." He took hold of her arms, closing his fingers around her soft flesh. "He's not me anymore. I don't want to remember him."

"Dirk—"

"I've spoken with Indigo, Shane. I've seen her." He pulled her with him back into the living room and sat down beside her on the couch. "You were right. She opened up a world for me that I shut my eyes to long ago. I didn't tell you before. I couldn't. But she wrote me dozens of letters after she left. I was too hurt and too proud to answer them. My mother wrote, too, and I threw her letters in the ocean, unopened, believing with a child's reasoning that I was loyal to my father."

"Oh, Dirk."

"What I told you about not feeling anything for my mother wasn't true in the beginning. The day she and Indigo left, I ran after them down to the wharf, crying, begging them not to go, throwing handsful of sand in the cotton buyer's face. I vowed then to keep Wanatoka free from thieving strangers forever. And I never forgave them."

"But you still loved Indigo and your mother," Shane said in a whisper.

"Loved them. And hated them. Indigo told me my mother stayed with her friend for less than a month. She never remarried. All the time I was furious at her for not acknowledging my father's death, she was dead herself, five years before him, in a cheap little rooming house where she took in sewing."

Tears streamed down Shane's face. "I'm so sorry, Dirk."

"So am I—for all the years I wasted feeling angry and then not being able to feel anything at all. If you hadn't come along—"

"Have you forgiven me?"

"For what?" His voice thickened. "For being the sun and the rain that started me growing again? You brought life back to me—and I let you get away."

She reached out for his hands. "I was horrible that last day, horrible so many times before when

I tried to impose my will on you. You were right to call me rigid and prissily dutiful."

"I never called you prissy."

Shane smiled through her tears. "You should have, if you didn't." Her gaze moved out over the room. "I never knew myself until I was locked up in this apartment trying to finish my thesis and I saw finally how mixed up my values were."

He wiped at her tears with gentle fingers. "You weren't wrong in setting goals for yourself."

"I was wrong in worshiping them, in putting them above the dictates of my heart. I've regretted so many times turning my back on you when you asked me to be patient, to give you more time to discover love." Her voice broke. "I have a list a mile long of things I regret."

"So do I," he told her with matching hoarseness. "It might take me a lifetime to work all the way through it." He drew her closer. "Do you have a lifetime to spare, Shane?"

Her lips parted.

"I'm asking you to marry me."

"Dirk, oh, Dirk! Are you sure?"

"Sure that I love you, that I want you at my side forever?" He rained kisses on her wet cheeks. "I've never been surer of anything in my life. Why do you think I came back here tonight?"

Her breath caught in a half-sob. "To save Professor Mitterand from a stroke."

He laughed and wrapped her in his arms, his face buried in the soft swirls of her hair. "I came here to offer you everything I have in the world. Will you take it?"

"You know I will." She melted against him. "But all I really want is you."

His mouth came down and covered hers. So many times she had dreamed of being in his arms again. But her dreams were pale, sickly shadows compared to the reality of Dirk holding her, of his strength and his love flowing out to her through his lips, through his breath, through the hardening of his body molding hers.

He muttered hoarsely in her ear, "Is there a bedroom in this place?"

"I can't remember." She clung to him. "I can't think of anything except that you love me."

He found his own way and lay down with her, lifting off the crepe-de-chine dress, hurrying with her shoes and then her stockings. And then at last his clothes were off, too. The sleek lines of his body arched above her. With a glad cry of release Shane lifted to meet him.

Never had she felt more loved and fulfilled. The thrusting power of Dirk's presence within her set fire to her limbs and her blood and every pulsing cell that made her a woman. The new freedom coursing through her captivated Dirk, too, and together in successively heightened bursts of passion they rose out of all that had kept them prisoners of the past . . . rose into fields of flowers and singing birds and rippling streams . . . into the night sky, where stars flamed eternally and the cinders and ashes of burned-out dreams were merely myths.

Finally they were still again.

Shane said softly, "I haven't said yet that I love you."

Dirk moaned. "You have. But tell me again."

She moved her lips to his eyelids, to his forehead, to his chin. "Will you take me back to Wanatoka?"

He turned over and faced her. "Do you want to be married there?"

"Yes." She closed her eyes. "In the living room with the windows open to the sea and everyone we love listening to our vows. My parents. Indigo—" She sat up and looked at him. "Will Indigo come?"

He took her hands in his and kissed the soft undersides of her wrists. "She's there already, with her husband and her children. They're waiting to meet you."

"Oh, Dirk! How soon can we go?"

"Now. In the morning. Whenever you want. The plane is ready and waiting." He paused. "There's just one thing."

Shane's face clouded.

"Your teaching fellowship."

"Oh—" She sighed and leaned limply against him. "I don't have one."

He sat up abruptly, holding her away from him. "Do you mean that after all your work, all your pious dedication, all the agony you put me through, those idiots passed you by?"

Shane laughed at the angry flush spreading over his skin. "Not at all, my darling. They offered me four, in fact. But I turned them all down."

"Why?" he demanded.

Her glowing eyes moved tenderly over his craggy face. "I didn't know why until tonight, but now I understand." Leaning, forward, she kissed his lips. "Love was leading me home to you."

RAPTURE ROMANCE

**Provocative and sensual,
passionate and tender—
the magic and mystery of love
in all its many guises**

Coming next month

TELL US YOUR OPINIONS AND RECEIVE A FREE COPY
OF THE RAPTURE NEWSLETTER.

Thank you for filling out our questionnaire. Your response to the following questions will help us to bring you more and better books. In appreciation of your help we will send you a free copy of the Rapture Newsletter.

1. Book Title: _____

   Book # : _____ (5–7)

2. Using the scale below how would you rate this book on the following features? Please write in one rating from 0–10 for each feature in the spaces provided. Ignore bracketed numbers.

(Poor) 0 1 2 3 4 5 6 7 8 9 10 (Excellent)
                                    0–10 Rating

Overall Opinion of Book. . . . . _____ (8)
Plot / Story. . . . . _____ (9)
Setting / Location. _____ (10)
Writing Style. . . . . _____ (11)
Dialogue. . . . . _____ (12)
Love Scenes. . . . . _____ (13)
Character Development:
Heroine:. . . . . _____ (14)
Hero:. . . . . _____ (15)
Romantic Scene on Front Cover. . . . . _____ (16)
Back Cover Story Outline . . . . _____ (17)
First Page Excerpts. . . . . _____ (18)

3. What is your: Education: Age: _____ (20-22)

      High School (   )1   4 Yrs. College (   )3
      2 Yrs. College (   )2   Post Grad   (   )4 (23)

4. Print Name: _____

   Address: _____

   City: _____ State: _____ Zip: _____

   Phone # (   ) _____ (25)

Thank you for your time and effort. Please send to New American Library, Rapture Romance Research Department, 1633 Broadway, New York, NY 10019.

GET SIX RAPTURE ROMANCES EVERY MONTH FOR THE PRICE OF FIVE.

Subscribe to Rapture Romance and every month you'll get six new books for the price of five. That's an $11.70 value for just $9.75. We're so sure you'll love them, we'll give you 10 days to look them over at home. Then you can keep all six and pay for only five, or return the books and owe nothing.

To start you off, we'll send you four books absolutely FREE. "Apache Tears," "Love's Gilded Mask," "O'Hara's Woman," and "Love So Fearful." The total value of all four books is $7.80, but they're yours *free* even if you never buy another book.

So order Rapture Romances today. And prepare to meet a different breed of man.

YOUR FIRST 4 BOOKS ARE FREE! JUST PHONE 1-800-228-1888*

(Or mail the coupon below)
*In Nebraska call 1-800-642-8788

Rapture Romance, P.O. Box 996, Greens Farms, CT 06436

Please send me the 4 Rapture Romances described in this ad FREE and without obligation. Unless you hear from me after I receive them, send me 6 NEW Rapture Romances to preview each month. I understand that you will bill me for only 5 of them at $1.95 each (a total of $9.75) with no shipping, handling or other charges. I always get one book FREE every month. There is no minimum number of books I must buy, and I can cancel at any time. The first 4 FREE books are mine to keep even if I never buy another book.

Name	(please print)

Address	City

State	Zip	Signature (if under 18, parent or guardian must sign)

 **RAPTURE ROMANCE**

This offer, limited to one per household and not valid to present subscribers, expires June 30, 1984. Prices subject to change. Specific titles subject to availability. Allow a minimum of 4 weeks for delivery.

RAPTURE ROMANCE

*Provocative and sensual,
passionate and tender—
the magic and mystery of love
in all its many guises*

Buy them at your local
bookstore or use coupon
on next page for ordering.

RAPTURE ROMANCE

Provocative and sensual, passionate and tender— the magic and mystery of love in all its many guises

---

Buy them at your local bookstore or use this convenient coupon for ordering.

NEW AMERICAN LIBRARY

P.O. Box 999, Bergenfield, New Jersey 07621

Please send me the books I have checked above. I am enclosing $_____ (please add $1.00 to this order to cover postage and handling). Send check or money order—no cash or C.O.D.'s. Prices and numbers are subject to change without notice.

Name_____

Address_____

City _____ State _____ Zip Code _____

Allow 4-6 weeks for delivery.

This offer is subject to withdrawal without notice.

RAPTURE ROMANCE

*Provocative and sensual,
passionate and tender—
the magic and mystery of love
in all its many guises*

Buy them at your local

bookstore or use coupon

on last page for ordering.

RAPTURE ROMANCE

Provocative and sensual, passionate and tender— the magic and mystery of love in all its many guises

---

Buy them at your local bookstore or use coupon on next page for ordering.

ON SALE NOW!

Signet's daring new line of historical romances . . .

SCARLET RIBBONS

In the decadent world of Shanghai, her innocence and golden beauty aroused men's darkest desires. . . .

DRAGON FLOWER
by Alyssa Welles

Sarina Paige traveled alone to exotic Shanghai not knowing fate was sending her into the storm of rich American Janson Carlyle's lust. But even as his kisses awakened her passion, his demand for her heart without promising his own infuriated her.

Sarina's blonde beauty was a prize many men tried to claim, including the handsome Mandarin, Kwen, who offered her irresistible pleasures on his sumptuous estate and the warmth of his protective love. But Janson offered her the dream of fulfilling her deepest desires, and pursued by these two powerful men, she fought to choose her own destiny. . . .

(0451-128044—$2.95 U.S., $3.50 Canada)